A LITTLE WILDER

A STEAMY SMALL-TOWN ROMANTIC COMEDY

SERENA BELL

1

MARI

I'm awakened in the pitch dark by the unexpected press of warm bodies on either side of me and something wet probing my ear.

I scream.

They scream.

There's a lot more screaming. And... barking. And scrabbling, and the sound of something sliding off the bed onto the floor and yelping.

Which is super alarming because I live alone. Or, for now, I am staying alone.

The beings on either side of me start to cry.

Children! There are children in my bed! And that wet sensation in my ear, was that a... dog?

I touch my belly, totally irrationally, but yep—still pregnant. So the children are not mine.

I mean, assuming I'm in my right mind and haven't traveled in time.

Which—I am, and I haven't, right?

But I can be excused for wondering, can't I? Because *where did they all come from*?

"Mommy!" one of them shrieks. "Someone's sleeping in my bed!"

Holy shit. I'm Goldilocks.

Was there porridge?

I *swear*—there was no porridge.

Thoroughly disoriented in time and space, I start to pick through what I know. I don't get very far before I'm suddenly blinking into the bright overhead light.

A man and a woman stand just inside the door of my bedroom. The woman has her hand on the light switch.

Is this a home invasion? At... I check out the clock on the nightstand... 4:12 a.m.? An alien invasion?

Do they often bring small children with them?

Do they usually start the process by inserting the small children into your bed?

Because I'm in my own bed.

I am a hundred percent sure of that.

"What the fuuuuhhh..." the man breathes, before the woman, who is also blinking in the light's assault, says, "Honey!"

He cuts himself off.

As he strides forward, I shrink back. His hands snake out.

I yank the covers up to my eyes, like a four-year-old who has—well, just found someone in her bed. My free hand protectively cups my almost seven-month pregnant belly.

The man is coming ever closer in what feels like slow-mo, and my heart pounds, because even though children and small yappy dogs aren't particularly threatening, adult humans suddenly appearing in your bedroom for absolutely no reason are definitely grounds for freaking the hell out.

Now he looms over me, but instead of strangling me and leaving me for dead, he snatches the child closest to him and cradles her to his chest.

The woman hurries forward, her eyes never leaving mine, and grabs the crying toddler on my other side.

Dad. And Mom.

My heart slows down by a few thousand beats per minute.

"She's in my bed!" wails the child from her dad's arms, pointing at me accusingly.

"It's my bed!"

Whoops. I guess I'm not my best self when I get awakened before dawn by a probably benign home invasion.

Biting my lower lip, I sit up. The covers slip down a notch.

Maybe I was a little hasty in my assertion.

To be fair, it's *not* actually *my* bed.

Yeah, see. *This* is why. No matter how great people are about letting you bunk with them, it's not actually such a great idea.

The bed I'm in belongs to family friends, and I'm crashing here, in their garage apartment, while I finish out my pregnancy and deliver my baby. Because the bed that's really mine is in my early-nineties Airstream Classic mobile home, and is distinctly less comfortable for a pregnant woman than I would have guessed.

Go figure.

"Who *are* you?" the woman demands.

She doesn't look super threatening. She looks tired. And confused. She's probably mid-thirties, pale-skinned, with brown hair loose and frizzy. Her husband is a matched set to her. He has his free hand in a fist—but doesn't seem inclined to do anything with it. He's soft-bodied. Dad-bodied. And wide-eyed. Not super scary, even with the fist.

"Who are *you*?" I counter, trying to keep my voice gentle. You know, in case there's a perfectly reasonable explanation, which I'm really hoping there is.

"You first," the woman says. She squares her shoulders. Nope, still not very threatening.

I let the covers slip down to my chin and say, "I'm Marigold Barrymore. I'm John and Arlene's friend. They're letting me stay here."

"Oh, *wow*," whispers the woman, exchanging glances with her husband. "Um, like, for how long?"

"Until I pop," I say, lowering the covers to show her the situation.

Her eyes practically bug out of her head. "Oh, *wow*," she says again. "That's, um... Honey?"

She turns to her husband, communicating volumes to him with her eyes, none of it good. Then back to me. She bites her lip and does a little twist side to side like an uncertain preteen girl. "I'm their daughter, Suzy."

"Oh!" I say. "Suzy! And Rick! And the kids!" Although I thought Arlene said there were four kids. Could be my early-morning counting is off. "Arlene and John have told me so much about you!"

"Yeah." Suzy wrings her hands. "We, um, got this last-minute Airbnb client. The kids are homeschooled, plus

Rick and I work from home, so we decided to take a surprise trip to see Grammy and Gramps. We figured we'd drive all night so the kids could wake up here."

She looks down at the toddler still in her arms, and over at the sniffling child her husband is guarding. "Maybe not the most genius plan ever?" She bites her lip.

"I think it's sweet," I say, because in theory, I endorse the idea of surprise trips and driving all night and bringing family together.

It's just that this is a very small apartment. Galley kitchen, tiny living room with a couch, one bedroom with a double bed. And yeah, that's about it.

"How long were you planning to stay?" I ask.

"A month?" she whispers. "I'm—so sorry. I had no idea anyone was staying here. Dad never mentioned it on the phone. They just kept saying how much they missed us—we used to live close—and how it wasn't the same when they couldn't hang out with the kids."

She casts an anxious look at her husband.

"Honey," he says gently. "It's going to be fine. I promise. We can probably stay with my folks."

He steps forward and takes her hand. I melt a little. Yeah, they're definitely not serial-killer bed invaders. Just a family with nowhere to go at the moment.

A small voice behind them says, "Mom? We got scared waiting in the car, so we came in."

Two small kids, hand-in-hand, slip into the room and eye me with their own version of anxiety.

"Mom?" The obviously older one, who must be around eight, looks confused.

"Mommy?" The younger one's brown hair is a tangle,

and she's still blinking sleepily and clinging tight to her sister's hand.

"Who's that?" the oldest asks.

"That's Marigold. She's living here."

"If she's living here, where are we going to stay?" the oldest asks.

The two children burst into tears, drawing a sympathetic wail from the toddler on his mother's chest.

The baby inside me kicks. I slide out from under the covers.

"You're going to stay here," I say, and stand up to begin stripping the sheets from the bed.

Suzy stops me with a hand on my arm.

"But you're—"

Both parents' eyes fix on my belly.

I shake my head. "Your parents' couch is available, comfy, and just next door. I'll sneak in there tonight. I've already gotten six hours of good sleep. You've been driving all night with four kids. Get them settled, get some sleep, and we'll figure this whole thing out in the morning."

Suzy hesitates. I can tell she wants to refuse.

For a split second, I let myself want her to refuse. I let myself want a place to stay, a place to settle down, a place of my own.

Then I shake it off.

"Let me help you remake the bed," I offer, opening a small linen cupboard and finding the sheets she'll need. I start to hand the sheets to her, then realize she still has her arms full of toddler, and make the bed myself. She objects —"You're the pregnant one!"—but I wave her off, saying, "Yeah, the one with my hands still free."

When that's done, and I've said goodnight to everyone *and* the dog, I cross the gravel area from Arlene and John's garage apartment to their house. I let myself in with the spare key and wrap my sheet around the couch cushions as best I can. I drag Arlene's favorite blanket off her lounge chair, pull it over me, and close my eyes.

Arlene and John's couch is...

Well, it's well-loved. My butt—which has gotten a lot bigger lately—sinks down between the two sofa cushions and finds a hard bit of wood underneath.

My hips have all kinds of opinions lately, and they start weighing in on the situation. *Shift that way, Mari. Whoops. No, the other way. Ouch.*

I'm not supposed to sleep on my back. Left side is better, so I get up and walk around so I'm facing the other way. But that feels weird, too.

After what feels like hours, I finally accept that sleep isn't coming for me anytime soon and sit up, pulling my phone out from where I'd tucked it under the couch.

I do what I've done almost every night since the doctor showed me the results of my pregnancy blood test:

I search for him.

He told me so little about himself.

Almost nothing at all.

So I do the only thing I can, my image search. The night of our one-night stand in Vegas, he was wearing a t-shirt with a graphic on the front of Bigfoot skiing. Shortly after I discovered I was pregnant, I found a photo in an online store that looked like my memory of that shirt. Since then, I've been reverse image-searching it. My fantasy is that he'll wear the shirt, someone will photograph him and drop it on social media, and that same day, he'll pop up in my search. Then I'll reach out to him... just in case.

Just in case he wants the baby, I mean.

Not because I want to see him again.

I'm too pragmatic to want that.

And maybe a day will come when he does pop up in my reverse image search, but...

It is Not. This. Night. As Aragorn would say.

I give up, as I have approximately a hundred and fifty times before. And move on to reading adoptive parent profiles on the self-match adoption site I've been haunting.

We can't have a bio baby, but we can and will love your baby like our own...

Caring, thoughtful, steady...

Fun-loving, mischievous, sometimes sarcastic...

Two-professor household...

Arlene, who's an early riser, comes in. Her salt-and-pepper hair is a wild puff around her head. When she sees me on the couch, her eyes get big. "What—?"

"Your daughter and her family are here!" I announce it like it's an awesome surprise, because it is, for her.

"They're—what?"

"They got a last-minute Airbnb offer for their place."

"They kicked you out?"

Arlene is gratifyingly outraged, but I shake my head. "No—I offered to come over here. There are six of them. It only makes sense."

"Gosh, I'm so sorry!" She reaches for her phone, which is charging on the side table, and scans the screen. "Oh, man, look at that. I must've just missed their text when I turned in early. Geez, that must've been a fright!"

I tell her the story, and we both laugh at the picture of me waking up to find three warm critters in my bed.

"I wish I could have seen your face!" she says, snorting, then sobers up. "Still, I'm really sorry! You know you're absolutely welcome to the couch for as long as you need it. And they'll be out of there in a couple of days, right?"

"Mmm," I say vaguely. Suzy will sort her out later this morning.

A month.

It's not the end of the world. I'm sure I'll get used to the couch. And if not, I can go back to sleeping in the Airstream.

My hips deliver a mean-ass monologue about that, but I ignore them.

Arlene points to the phone in my hands. "Were you looking at profiles again?"

"Yeah," I admit. Arlene is my late aunt's friend. She knows my childhood history, and she knows that when I can't sleep, I search the profiles.

"Any luck?"

"Uh. I mean, yeah. A few look good."

Arlene lifts her graying eyebrows so they almost meet her bangs. Right now she's wearing a ratty pink terry robe, and looks like a grandma in a TV ad. Those people sleeping in my bed—I mean, their bed, obviously—are lucky to have her.

"Nothing, huh?" Arlene says. Not really a question.

Arlene knows the problem isn't really with the families. It's...

Well, it's something else.

Three months ago, right after I got to San Bernardino,

where John and Arlene live, I made an appointment with an adoption counselor. A friend of a friend of Arlene's, actually.

To find someone to adopt your unborn baby, our counselor will review profiles with you and help you find a family that meets your criteria. This process can be enjoyable with the right counselor! the website proclaimed.

It said a lot of other things, too. Like you should make sure you're certain you want to find an adoption placement before you make an appointment.

Taking into account the absence of Bigfoot guy, I was certain.

I'd been on the road for the last ten years, following my impulses, picking up work as an RV interior designer where I could.

After all, I'd grown up on the road with a mom who never meant to have me and had definitely not thought through how much her life would change when she did—if not immediately, then when I was a teenager.

A baby needed a mom who was committed to the job. Stability—financial, emotional, and—to an extent— geographical. A real home.

Like my mother, I wasn't that mom. Wasn't that *person*.

Bigfoot guy was still MIA and, yes, I was *certain*. I thought.

I made and canceled four appointments.

It wasn't exactly a conscious decision. Things kept coming up. Arlene's dentist had a last-minute opening for a filling. Arlene mentioned that her closet desperately needed organizing, so I spent a day helping her create some tidy built-ins, double rods, and other solutions. The diner where I work called me in for an extra shift—and then offered me bonus money since it was last-minute. Not gonna turn that down, right?

The last appointment I canceled?

I had a paper cut. Or maybe it was a canker sore. Or an ingrown hair? I can't remember.

Arlene watches me quietly, maybe even sympathetically, and I don't want to get into it with her. I do the pretending-my-phone-buzzed-in-my-lap thing. And it turns out I have a notification of a direct message in Instagram, where I get most of my job inquiries from, because I am pretty active on the Airstream hashtags. I tap through.

Huh.

Arlene notices. "What?"

"I just got a cool request-for-proposal. Some guy has six Airstream trailers he's renovating to create an"—I quirk my fingers—"upscale camping experience. But he needs me ASAP."

"Where?"

"Near Bend, Oregon. Some town called Rush Creek."

I can already picture the trip, laid out on the map in my head. I-5 to San Francisco—where I can stop and see friends—U.S. 101 from San Fran to Crescent City, and then U.S. 199 to Bend. 199 is narrow and winding, not to mention landslide territory if it rains, but the other options are no prize either, this time of year.

I get the tingle of anticipation that always goes with route planning, a tingle that turns quickly into an impulse, a need to move.

And it's not just that. My Airstream, Bernadette, will need a new transmission in the next year or two. She needs to be re-waterproofed. And her electrical system—well, if you know anything about Airstreams, I don't need to explain. There's a *lot* of deferred maintenance on Bernadette.

A job like the one this guy is presenting would definitely let me *un*defer that maintenance, which is super appealing.

"Mari?" Arlene must have noticed I've gone somewhere in my head.

"Do you remember the road trip my mom and I took the summer I was fifteen?"

She nods.

"We did Western Canada on that trip. The weather was phenomenal that summer, perfect. But the day we were headed to Lake Louise, it started pouring. Pouring. My mom insisted we'd made a wrong turn and made me study the map again, and she was right. When we got back to the turnoff we'd missed and got on the right road, the rain instantly stopped. And you know what my mom said?"

Arlene shakes her head.

"She started laughing and said, 'We were on someone else's vacation! We took a wrong turn and got on someone else's vacation!' And I just never forgot that. That if the weather's bad, sometimes you have to find the road you were supposed to be on."

Her face is all scrunched up in confusion.

I try again. "I'm saying, maybe my wakeup last night was literal. Like, the universe telling me I was in the wrong bed. In the wrong place."

Arlene squints at me. "Or maybe," she says dryly, "my

daughter is a little inconsiderate and not great about planning ahead?"

Just then—as if she's summoned Suzy—there's a disturbance at the front door and Suzy and the kids pour into Arlene's living room. With cries of "Grammy!" the kids throw themselves on Arlene, who beams hugely, hugs everyone, and takes the littlest one from Suzy. It's a whirlwind of family love and energy.

Something I never had and never learned to want. And yet right now, watching them, I feel a twinge of...

Longing.

Cooing at the toddler, Arlene herds her family into the kitchen and starts whipping up breakfast for them. From the next room, I can hear them bouncing around, like popcorn kernels in an air popper.

A moment later, Arlene cries, "Mari! Get in here! I'm making French toast. You don't want to miss it!"

I get. I join them. I eat Arlene's absolutely amazing French toast. I laugh with Suzy, and I make kiddo chit-chat with the little ones.

But I feel like an extra in the scene, and as breakfast goes on, the conviction grows in me. I was right. The universe woke me up in the middle of the night last night to get my attention.

To make sure that when the guy with the six trailers in Rush Creek sent me that email—I'd see it for what it was.

A map.

It's time to hit the road.

2

───────

KANE

Something's not right.

Veronica's parents are acting weird.

When I show up this morning for my weekly Friday morning visit, they don't have their usual list of tasks for me.

Instead, they invite me in for a cup of coffee and some teacakes.

Veronica's mom, Sigrid, keeps giving me these nervous looks. And Frank, Veronica's dad, won't meet my eyes at all.

I know what to do in these situations, though. I'm the fourth of five brothers—plus our sister Amanda—so six kids. I've spent a lifetime learning that if you don't know what's going on, you should sit down, shut the fuck up, and open your ears and eyes until you can get the lay of the land. Then, and only then, can you figure out how to fix whatever's gone wrong. Patch it up. Smooth it over. Peacemake the *shit* out of it. So I listen.

Sigrid, Frank, and I have been talking about the

weather for the last fifteen minutes or so. Admittedly, that is a subject of super close interest to me right now. But still.

"So they're not making any snow?" Frank says.

"On the lower mountain, a little," I tell him. "But it's not like you can make a whole backcountry's worth of snow if the weather decides to make this the worst snow season in the region's history."

"Makes sense," Frank says.

Both he and Sigrid are in their late seventies, and not in the greatest health. Frank lost a lot of mobility last year after a stroke. He can get around, but mostly with a walker. Sigrid has emphysema, and gets winded with the slightest exertion. So ever since Veronica and I got serious about each other, a few months ago, I've been coming over to their house to help out with anything I can—changing light bulbs, fixing minor plumbing issues, cleaning out the garage. It was my idea.

It started when Veronica mentioned that she worried nonstop about her parents staying put in their house, instead of moving into assisted living, and that she'd thought about hiring in-home care, but it was expensive, and her parents were stubborn. They didn't want her to pay someone to put a safety railing in the bathtub! she told me, getting agitated.

I offered to install the bath bar. No big deal. The Wilder brothers may be outdoorsmen, but we were brought up to repair anything that needs fixing. So there aren't too many around-the-house issues this handyman can't tackle.

When I was installing the bath bar, I noticed that the tile needed regrouting, so I took that on. Then Sigrid asked if I could help her post some items for sale and giveaway online, since I'm a photographer. I was pleased to be useful, and didn't fess up to her that it doesn't take any special skill —or even my Nikon—to take those photos. And, well—the rest is history. I'm happy to help with repairs, and Sigrid is happy to bake for me.

Bonus: Veronica always thanks me for my efforts with lots of enthusiasm.

"Are you sure there isn't anything I can do for you guys today?" I ask. As much as I enjoy Frank and Sigrid, I'm so tired of talking about this disaster of a ski season that I'd rather watch *The Fault in Our Stars* again.

Frank and Sigrid exchange looks. The small ball of unease in my belly turns into a thorny tangle of nettles. This has to be bad. Grim health news from Sigrid's Monday visit to the pulmonologist maybe. Or Frank had another small stroke—he's had a series of minor ones since the big one last year.

"Kane," Sigrid says gently. "We have something to tell you. We hate to be the bearers of bad news."

Oh, shit. Cancer. Alzheimer's. Veronica will be crushed. I wonder if she already knows? It's strange that this news would come from her parents and not from her—but maybe they want me to help cushion the blow. Maybe they want me to be with her when they tell her—so they need to prime me first.

"Veronica wanted to tell you herself. She really did. But she's not very good if she thinks there's going to be conflict. She's—she's actually terrible at conflict."

Sigrid and Frank exchange another look, and my brain desperately, and unsuccessfully, tries to keep up with this new twist.

Sigrid sucks in a deep breath. "She really cares about you, Kane. But it's just not working for her."

Wait.

Wait a fucking second.

"Are you *breaking up* with me?" I demand.

No. This is not a thing. Adult women in their thirties do *not* have their parents break up with their boyfriends for them.

I must be misunderstanding.

But I am not misunderstanding. Sigrid is nodding, her expression tragic, her hand reaching for mine on the table. Covering mine.

"You're so unbelievably *kind*, Kane. Everything you've done for Veronica. For *us*. She told us how much you want marriage and kids, how your brothers are starting to pair off and you want that too. She couldn't bear to see the hurt on your face when she told you."

I jerk my hand away. "I'm not *hurt*," I say—not stopping to think about whether this is true, because self-preservation demands I say it no matter what. "I'm pissed. I'm pissed because who has their *parents* break up for them? I thought text messages were as low as it got!"

"She didn't want to break up with you by text," Sigrid says, in a *God-forbid* tone.

"Well, right," I say. "Because that would be a dick move!" I am no longer watching my language, because we have left the reality zone and transported straight to Nopesville.

"Kane," Sigrid says. She's trying to be soothing.

I close my eyes.

"Part of why we all thought it would be a good idea for

this news to come from us and not from Veronica is that Frank and I want to continue having a relationship with you."

Her hand creeps over mine again.

"We've loved getting to know you, Kane," Sigrid says. "We've loved having your help around the house. We don't want to lose all that, just because Veronica is looking for someone a little more... driven."

"Driven," I repeat.

"Someone who isn't a ski bum," Frank supplies, obviously trying to be helpful.

"I'm not a ski bum," I say, as calmly as I can.

"Well, you do ski for a living," Sigrid offers.

"I lead ski trips for a living," I correct.

Sigrid squints at me. "Not this winter so much, though."

"Because there's no snow." It grinds out of my clenched jaw. This is the worst snow winter in the Bend area in recorded history, and the mountain is a patchy mess. We're talking act-of-God mess.

"Kane." Sigrid's voice is super gentle as she reaches across the table and pats my hand again. "You're the nicest guy Veronica's ever brought home. You're thoughtful, handy, kind—you're basically the boy-next-door we always dreamed she'd fall for."

Nicest.

Kind.

The boy next door.

How many times have I heard some version of that—as the prelude to or reason for a breakup?

I close my eyes and think about Veronica. She's very pretty, with long, straight, honey-blond hair, and hazel eyes.

She's medium-height and just the right amount of curvy to feel sturdy under my hands. She likes movies and concerts and mystery novels, and we often order takeout so we can Netflix and chill. The sex is good. Well, decent.

I try to think if there's anything else I can say about Veronica.

She has a cute dog. Actually, I freaking love that dog.

If I'm being honest with myself, I'd been thinking that if Veronica and I stayed serious and moved in together, I'd get to see the dog a lot more often.

And yes, I'd fantasized about marriage and kids.

Maybe more than I'd fantasized about Veronica herself.

What the *hell* have I been doing?

What the hell *am* I doing with my life?

All I know is that it isn't this.

It can't possibly have come to this, to my girlfriend's parents breaking up with me and me feeling worse about the loss of my imaginary kids than the loss of my real live girlfriend.

For a split second I remember Vegas. When I wasn't the boy next door. When I wasn't sensible, responsible... or even kind, unless you want to give me credit for making sure the woman with me came first. Which... no. Since making sure both partners get off is the minimum requirement for decent sex, no one should be taking bonus points for it.

My heart rate kicks through the ceiling at the memory.

That sex? That sex wasn't decent or even good....

It was mind-blowing.

But that wasn't you, a voice argues in my head.

Well, maybe I want it to be, I argue back.

What happens in Vegas stays in Vegas, the voice retorts.

That doesn't mean I have to ride this train to bananas town.

"Kane?" Sigrid interrupts my inner monologue.

"Sorry," I say. "I gotta go. And, um, although I super much appreciate your willingness to friend zone me? I'm gonna take a raincheck on that."

They look a little confused. Which is understandable. They're not qualified to break up with their daughter's boyfriend. It's not in their skill set. I clarify. "No thank you on the staying friends with you guys. I appreciate the offer. But no thank you."

Sigrid looks startled. But then her face softens into a sad smile. "We get it, Kane, we do. It's asking a lot. But we had to try."

Frank sticks out a hand. Shakes mine.

And, let's face it, for better or for worse, I am the boy next door. I have some flaws, but being mean isn't one of them.

"Frank," I say, shaking back. "If you're really in a pinch with repair stuff, let me know and I can take a crack at whatever it is."

And, crossing the kitchen, I tip my coffee down the drain, toss the rest of my teacake into the trash, and—carefully setting my dishes in the sink—let myself out the front door.

I pause on the front stoop, noting a crack in the slate that could become a tripping hazard for Frank and Sigrid.

I'll come back next week and patch it.

The boy next door has left the building, but you can't take the boy next door out of the man.

I DRAG my sorry ass to work, where I'm greeted with chaos. My family runs an outdoor adventuring business—Wilder Adventures. Right now, three of my brothers, plus our co-worker Hanna, my brother Gabe's wife, Lucy, and my mom, Barb, are heatedly arguing around the table.

"The thing is," Gabe says sternly—he says pretty much everything sternly, because he's the big boss and also just bossy—"It's never as good when they do half and half."

"I agree," my mom says. She often backs Gabe's play, so this isn't shocking. I think she's still trying to get back in his good graces after she hired Lucy behind his back to revamp the business he's basically run since he was fifteen. It was a pretty low blow, sure... but on the other hand, it resulted in him—and us—gaining Lucy, so actually no one is complaining.

"I feel like they always skimp. It's like if you can't commit, they punish you by holding back on both."

"I just feel like no one ever takes my vote seriously," my youngest brother Easton says.

"Your nickname is Easton the Panty Melter," Hanna says. "No one can take you seriously."

In addition to being a close family friend, Hanna's my partner in the ski trips, and one of my best friends. She's also Easton's opposite. Like matter and anti-matter opposites. It still feels miraculous to me every time they're both in the same room and the universe keeps spinning. Or expanding. Whatever it does. Not a science guy.

I hold a hand up. "Hey, everyone. Can I help here?"

They all turn to look at me, and I swear, their faces all

go clear, like I've just swept away the stress. Honestly, that is gratifying after the morning I've had. Veronica may not appreciate me, but my family definitely does.

"Kane," Gabe says sternly. See note above on *sternly*. But the thing about Gabe is, he's an armored nuclear sub filled with puppies and kittens—terrifying on approach, until you catch sight of the cargo. "See if you can get them to see reason on this. It would be so much better to get three larges with one topping on each pizza than to get six different toppings."

Oh. Pizza.

Yeah. This is a job for Super Kane, definitely.

"I got this," I say, holding out a hand. Gabe hands me the notebook and pen he was holding. "But wait—where's Amanda?"

Usually my only sister, who's a caterer, makes lunch for us.

"She got called for a last-minute lunch catering job. There was a cancellation and it's a big company so lots of potential business down the line. And she was short staffed, so she had to be on site."

"Got it. Pizza orders. Easton." I start with him, because if someone isn't feeling heard, it's a good idea to let them speak first. And no, I've never taken any kind of mediation course or anything. My family life *is* a mediation course.

"Hawaiian."

I note it. "Hanna."

"Anything with meat, but fruit on pizza, or touching my half of a pizza, is not okay." She glares at Easton. He glares back.

"Gabe."

"Pepperoni."

"Brody."

Brody is the Wilder family's resident bad boy. Or maybe it's more precise to say he's our former bad boy, since he's been heavily reformed since he fell for his fiancée, Rachel.

"Supreme."

"Mom."

"Mushroom. But as long as it doesn't have onions, I'm fine."

"Lucy?"

"Anything vegetarian."

I quickly sketch out three pizzas, then push the notebook across the table. With my pen as a pointer, I explain my reasoning.

"One half-Hawaiian, half Supreme. Because neither Easton nor Brody is concerned about how half-pizzas are inferior to whole pizzas, amirite?" I point the pen at both of them, and they nod.

I point to the next slightly lopsided round. "One pepperoni pizza, unsullied by having to share its surface with any other topping, for Gabe, Hanna, and Mom, since she's in the no-halfsies camp and her only hard rule is no onions."

"Slick," Brody says, admiringly.

"And"—I point to the third pizza—"one half mixed veggie, half mushroom, for Lucy, and Mom, if she wants to indulge her mushroom craving, even if it means a subpar topping-to-pizza ratio."

They are all silent.

"Can I take that as a yes?" I ask.

Nods all around.

"Thank you, Kane," my mother says, giving me big grateful Mama eyes. Take my word for it, that's a thing.

"Kane, you're a saint. I'll call it in," Lucy says, reaching for her phone. A moment later, she's relaying the order.

I exhale and relax. Another peacekeeping mission fulfilled.

As everyone scatters to get in a few minutes of work before the food arrives, I pull out my camera to snap photos. I've gotten in the habit of doing it whenever I can, because every once in a while I'll come up with something that's great for social media. Like right now, Easton is checking life jackets and paddles for wear, so I snap a few of him, because whenever a photo of Easton goes up on Instagram, we get bookings. Plus, of course, it's never a bad thing to emphasize how seriously we take safety.

My mother comes up next to me. "Kane," she says. "That pizza order."

"Uh-oh," I say. "What did I forget?"

She frowns at me, and I quickly race back through the conversation to make sure I didn't ignore anyone's prefer- ence. Nope, all good.

"You never said what kind of pizza you wanted."

I hadn't. Because I hadn't bothered to figure it out. It would just be one more constraint to add to the order, and all the choices sounded fine with me.

I open my mouth to say so, but at that exact moment, every phone in the room buzzes. That would be the family chat. We all grab for them, and immediately, all eyes turn to me.

Clark has texted: *I need Kane in Hott office ASAP.*

We all look at each other. Clark is...

Well, Clark is not prone to texting the whole family when he needs just one person. Or using the phrase "ASAP."

What's up? I text back, then add: *At headquarters. Can be there in ten.*

Just come.

Everyone's looking at me.

On my way.

3

KANE

The "Hott office" is, in fact, a Wilder trailer parked on Hanna's granddad—Mr. Hott's—land. It's cold, bare, and full of tasks I loathe. Unfortunately, because of the miserable snow-less ski season, it's where I've spent a lot of the last few weeks, making fruitless phone call after phone call.

That's probably what Clark wants from me, I'm thinking, as I pull up a few hundred feet from the trailer and park.

"Kane!"

Clark comes pounding up to the car. He's run out to meet me. What the hell? He's one of the steadiest, most unflappable people I know—the guy you want with you in an emergency. I've seen him set broken limbs, tourniquet wounds, give CPR, and treat snake bites. Even when his wife Emma died two-and-a-half years ago, he was calm—preternaturally so—pale, drawn, frozen, grieving, but iron-nerved.

I open the door to step out, but Clark holds up a hand.

"Kane, you're—wait. Hang on. No. Just stay there. You probably should be sitting down. Fuck. I don't even know where to start."

"Clark," I say, alarmed. "Jesus. It's not Jessa, is it?" Jessa is Clark's girlfriend.

"No, she's fine." That seems to snap him back to himself, and he takes a deep breath. "Okay. So. I did a thing." He casts me a pleading glance—which is also unusual for Clark. Clark doesn't *plead*. He just *does*. "And you're going to be mad. Like—really mad."

I shake my head. "I doubt that." I can't think of a time I got really mad at any of my brothers. Mildly irritated, of course. Genuinely angry? No.

I mean, aside from the time Easton replaced my Gatorade with Jell-o during a basketball game. And I probably wouldn't have been so angry if he'd let it solidify completely...

But Clark's not Easton. And his agitation is definitely unnerving.

I unfold myself from the car and step out, shutting the door behind me. "Come on, Clark, what is it?"

He's pacing now, which does nothing to calm the unsettled feeling in my gut. "I'm just going to give you the background. You'll have to see for yourself—it's not my place..."

I have no idea what he's talking about, and my heart is pounding now. "Spit it out, dude—you're scaring me."

He rakes a hand through his hair, standing it on end. "Okay, so, well, you know how bad it is with the trailer reno. I mean, we've called, what, like, everyone in the country, practically. Or that's what it feels like. So I..." He shakes his head, pulling his phone out of his pocket and handing it to me through the car window.

When I see the screen, I almost drop it.

I look up at him, my mouth hanging open.

"Yup," he says.

It's her.

I'm looking at an Instagram account, @AirstreamReimagined. This particular photo is of a woman standing outside a 90s-era Airstream Classic motorhome. She's petite, as slim and ethereal as a fairy, and topped with a mane of fiery red hair. Just looking at her makes my chest and my cock ache. I recognize the ache as longing.

"What the fuck, Clark?" I'm pissed because I've been trying to let what happened in Vegas stay right fucking where it happened, in the Bellagio lobby bar and bathroom. "I told you not to look for her."

He hangs his head and backs off a step, holding up his hands. "I know, Kane, I know, and I'm—I'm so fucking sorry. I just didn't know what else to do. If this renovation doesn't get done in time, we're going to lose all that income. I won't meet my numbers. Wilder won't meet its numbers. And that means we're going to have to cut back some of our spring plans for a year from now."

Right, right, right. Clark has to renovate six Airstream trailers in time for the fall camping season. He thought he was on schedule but a month ago, his chosen designer took a more lucrative job doing movie trailers for some epic television production in Saskatchewan. Since then, Clark and I have been searching for someone else to take the job—with no luck.

Now it's urgent—which I assume is why Clark ignored

my request and tracked down the woman in the Instagram post.

"How'd you find her?"

"She was mentioned in a thread on one of the Airstream forums. Apparently, she's killer at what she does. And as soon as I saw her name, I knew. Marigold. Marigold Barrymore."

Marigold.

It fits. The bright chaotic flare of her hair. The wild energy that burned through me that night. I wouldn't have expected her to turn out to be a Lily or a Rose.

Marigold.

We met while I was in Vegas for Gabe's bachelor party. We didn't exchange names, because we were both under the spell of Vegas magic and thought it would be fun to try out the sex-with-a-stranger fantasy, which neither of us had ever done. It seemed like a great idea at the time...

Only I couldn't forget her afterwards.

And that would have been that, a single night followed by a lifetime of frustrated longing. Except that afterwards, Clark and I realized that the night before Marigold rocked my world, Clark had also met her. Their conversation, thankfully, was purely professional—about the fact that Clark was renovating some Airstreams, which happened to be Marigold's specialty.

Marigold's business card had long since disappeared into the belly of Gabe's dog, and all Clark could remember was that her name was a flower. Edible, he thought.

I made him swear not to try to find her, because I had promised: What happens in Vegas stays in Vegas.

And now he's tracked her down.

I take a deep breath. Right. Clark's right. This isn't about me and how I did something totally out of character, or how much I liked it. In the scheme of things, that's not even a big deal. So I fucked a woman I'd never met, while pretending to be a type of person I wasn't, in a way that—after the fact—seemed insanely risky. So what?

It doesn't mean I have to let my mistake torpedo the family business.

I square my shoulders. "Okay. So... what... you're going to get in touch with her?"

Clark winces.

"You got in touch with her," I guess.

He lets out a slightly wounded sound. "Uh. Worse?"

"How much worse exactly?"

"Well, she's... here."

"Oh, fuck, Clark, are you serious? When were you going to tell me?"

He hangs his head again.

"You weren't going to tell me." I suck air into my lungs. "Okay. Okay. Look, this doesn't have to be a big deal, right? I'll just, you know, avoid her."

"Um. Well. That might not be such a good idea."

"What are you saying?"

"I'm saying—"

I have literally never seen my brother look that worried.

"Clark? I really need you to tell me what the fuck is going through your head right now."

But instead of answering, Clark says, "Come with me."

"Dude, no. Come on. I don't want to see her if I don't have to."

"You have to."

He puts his hands on my shoulders and steers me. It's then that I notice there's another Airstream parked near the trailers. An early 90s Classic. The motorhome model, not a trailer.

A woman stands in its side door. She's facing away from me, and even so, I recognize her right away. That petite, slender body, the mane of untamable red hair. She's wearing a gauzy tunic top and a flowing, flowery skirt, and even in the baggy clothes, she still looks delicate. I remember worrying that I'd hurt her, that she was fragile enough to break.

That was part of what drove me wild. Because she wasn't fragile. Not at all. She was hungry and strong. Flexible, firecracker eager, and insatiable.

And I'm flashing back to the rest of it. To her wide, soft mouth, her lithe little body, ultra-alive under my hands. She liked being held down, bossed around. She told me so, and I could feel it for myself, too.

Great. I'm going to greet her with a hard-on. Perfect first impression.

Second. Second impression.

Come to think of it, it's almost a habit at this point.

She turns around, and every thought goes out of my head. And the breath flies out of my lungs. I stand there, empty and stunned.

She's pregnant.

4

KANE

My brain goes into deep freeze. Some kind of shock setting, where everything happens in super slow-mo.

She starts to step down from the Airstream, onto the fold-out metal stairs.

She looks out as she does. Sees me. Her mouth opens. Her eyes get big.

She says, "You?"

And then she sways. Her foot catches the edge of the step, and she flails, her eyes opening even wider in alarm—

I react without thinking, lunging for her. Catching her before she can topple, pulling her body against mine to brace it. My arms are full of her, this woman I've tried to forget. All the details come flooding back. How she smells: bold, bright, almost but not quite citrusy, like the crushed petals of something strong but not exactly floral.

Like marigolds, I think.

How she feels. Still so light in my arms, like she isn't

quite human. Some kind of fairy or nymph, I don't know, something ethereal.

Her curves are full blown against me. Her breasts, which had been small enough to easily palm the night we fucked, the round of her belly—they're pressed so close that my body gives up trying not to react to her. I'm hard, and in the chaos of her—so soft here and so taut there and still struggling to right herself—I'd have to guess that despite my best efforts, she can feel what she instantly, easily does to me.

Yikes, that's a greeting.

I steady her and pull back, because even though we have a history, I don't think shoving my erection against her on first re-meeting is the right way to make a second impression.

But the touch of her body and the scent of her skin lingers even when I put space between us. I back up several steps until I collide with Clark, who steadies me with a hand on my shoulder.

Marigold is staring at me like she's seen a ghost. And now that the rescue's accomplished, I'm staring at her, because—

I don't know pregnant women very well.

I don't know exactly how to judge *how* pregnant they are.

But it takes nine months, right? And you don't show for the first three. And she's not huge-huge. She's medium-sized. So that means, she's... well, like, probably? About? Six or seven months pregnant.

I do some super-quick math.

It could be mine.

It could easily be mine.

Holy shit.

But... wait...

It could be someone else's, too.

I don't know anything about her. Maybe she has sex with strangers in Vegas hotel bathrooms regularly.

I hate that idea. I hate it with an unholy passion.

I want it to be mine.

Wait. What the hell...? Do I mean that?

I can't mean that.

But I hate the alternative so much that I think maybe I do.

I drag my gaze up from her lovely round belly, meaning to jump straight to eye contact, but I get stuck on the way. Just for a split second, but *wow*. Her breasts are a fucking thing of beauty. I cannot tear my eyes away.

She clears her throat, and my gaze snaps back up to meet hers. There's an expression on her face I can't read. I could be her dream come true or her worst nightmare.

And I realize I'm a complete disaster. I'm standing in front of this woman who I haven't been able to stop thinking about for months. Who is definitely pregnant with a child that might be mine. And despite the gravity of the moment, I haven't managed one word.

In fact, the first Wilder brother to speak is Clark.

"I'll, uh, leave you two to, um, chat," he says.

Instinctively, I grab for his arm. Like, *omigod, don't leave me, brother!*

"Kane," he murmurs. "You can do this. You *got* this." Then he gives me an unreadable look. "Also," he says, still under his breath. "I, um, know you have a lot going on here.

Like, a lot. But it would be awesome if you didn't fuck up the job situation. We need her."

That gets my attention.

Right.

As terrifying as this situation is, I know a few things. And one of them is that Wilders don't run.

Not from anything.

And definitely not from this.

For one thing, Wilder Adventures needs someone to redesign those Airstream trailers. That someone is Marigold, regardless of whose baby is rounding her belly like a basketball.

And if the baby is mine, then...

All the more reason not to run.

I want that baby to be mine.

This time I find it a little easier to admit it to myself.

I want the baby to be mine for all the reasons I tried to make things work out with Veronica. Because I crave back-yard wiffle ball and flag football and Capture the Flag games. Because I long for family vacations and Wilder parties where my kids run in packs with their cousins.

But I also want the baby to be mine in a primal way that makes it clear that wanting a happily ever after from Veronica is the romantic equivalent of settling for whatever pizza topping happens to land in front of you.

I want that baby to be mine because I haven't been able to get Marigold out of my head in the seven months since we walked away from each other. And now that I've seen her?

My whole self remembers why.

Clark gives my shoulder one last reassuring pat and

melts back toward the office, leaving the two of us alone. She's still standing on the ground just in front of the trailer.

I finally suck air into my lungs. I take a few steps toward her and manage, "Hi."

"Hi," she says.

One thing I *do* know about pregnancy, you're not supposed to comment on it unless the woman says something first. But not being able to comment on something that big and obvious and... *right there between us...* basically means that I can't form any other words.

And when I finally manage, what I say is,

"So. You're here about the trailers."

5

———————

MARI

I draw the first full breath I've been able to manage since I looked up to see him, and start to laugh. Because trailer talk was *so* not what I expected to come out of his mouth.

"Seriously?" I demand. "That's what you want to say to me?"

His mouth opens. And closes. And opens again.

"Uh," he says. "Uh. Not really."

We're facing each other. Standing maybe six feet apart, a chunk of that space taken up by my belly.

I'm still trying to pull myself back together. I'd like to say I just tripped on Bernadette's steps, but honestly? I got a little weak-kneed from surprise and relief when I saw him. And then? When he pulled me into his arms? I pretty much dropped straight into a hard-core flashback of that night. His big body pressing me into the wall, him turning me, holding my hands over my head so he could line up his iron-hard erection against my ass. Him bending me over the couch, telling me he wasn't going to come until I did, no matter how long I needed.

Whoops. Here come the weak knees again.

He doesn't seem to be able to pull himself out of his stunned moment, either. We're just staring at each other. I can't be sure what he's thinking, but I'm thinking about how once I say it out loud—"it's yours"—everything's going to change.

It's how I felt when the doctor came back into the exam room and said, *I have the results of your blood test.* I knew, just from looking at her face, that the next words out of her mouth would change everything. *Once she tells me,* I thought, *there's no going back.*

There's no going back.

There never was.

I say it quickly, like ripping off a band-aid.

"I'm pregnant. And it's yours."

And then, quick, because he looks like he's going to pass out, "Don't freak out."

"I'm not freaking out." He gives a short, pained laugh. "I mean, I'm sort of freaking out, but I'm—I'm... it's just a lot to absorb."

"I know the feeling," I say wryly. "That's how I was when I found out."

His eyes are darting back and forth like his mind's going a million miles per hour, which it probably is.

I've changed everything for him, just like the doctor's words did for me.

But finding him—or really, stumbling into him, because it's pretty obvious even Clark had no idea what he was setting in motion—changes everything again. Suddenly this baby has a dad, and I'd given up on that whole possibility.

Except it's also possible it changes nothing.

I wish he would say something. Even something angry.

It occurs to me he might doubt my story.

"If it helps," I tell him, "I'm happy to do a paternity test. There's a safe way, where they do this thing with fetal blood cells in my bloodstream. I don't actually expect you to take my word for anything. We knew each other, what, an hour?"

He nods distractedly. He's—not angry, I don't think. His expression is just sort of frozen and confused. Understandably.

"How...?" he asks. "You said you had an IUD."

"Yeah. I, um, had some weird bleeding, and I went to the doctor, and my IUD had ejected. It's pretty rare, but it happens. I never had periods with the IUD, so I didn't notice anything was weird. They did a pregnancy test and then an ultrasound... And voilà—there I was, more than three months pregnant. I weighed my options, which—it took some soul searching. But I made my choice, and..." I gesture to my belly. "Here I am."

Kane looks like he's about to interrupt, so I quickly add, "I tried to find you." I realize I haven't said that yet, and it's super important to me that he know that. "I did all these ridiculous searches, like 'hot guy with streaky hair, Bellagio.' I don't know what the hell I thought that would cough up, but needless to say, it didn't work. I also did a reverse image search on your shirt. That was basically the only thing I could think of that might work. The Bigfoot shirt," I explain.

He unbuttons the long-sleeved flannel shirt he's wearing and shows me the t-shirt underneath.

I smile. "Yeah. That one."

He rakes a hand through his hair—longish, gold-streaked, and—I remember—soft as silk. "So. You're pregnant. And it's mine. Wow. Um, wow."

I can't help it; I smile again. He's a lot dorkier than I remember. The guy who picked me up in Vegas was a smooth operator. I couldn't have imagined him going to pieces like this. He would have been wholly and totally in control of the whole conversation.

But this guy—he's just staring at me with an expression I can't quite read. It's not anger or even fear. It's almost like... reverence. Like I've done something marvelous.

And that can't be right, can it?

That makes less than no sense.

"Did you know?" he asks. "That I would be here?"

I shake my head. "I knew Clark had brothers. I even looked at the site, but I didn't—I didn't look closely. Because there was no reason to think that the guy I'd given my business card to one night in a hotel would turn out to be the brother of the guy I..." I stop.

I've never figured out what to call it exactly. In my head, sometimes I say *fucked*, but it doesn't feel quite right. Yeah, there were moments when it felt like that, in the best possible way. But there were also a lot of moments when it felt like something else. Like when he told me he wouldn't come until I did, but also that I should take my time, there was no rush.

Jesus...

When he caught me on the Airstream steps, he smelled

just like he had that night, when apparently I'd imprinted on him for my permanent scent preferences. Boy-next-door Ivory soap and grocery store apple-scented shampoo and Old Spice deodorant and the tang of male sweat under it, calling out to me in whatever musk language sweat uses to talk to our lizard brains.

I wanted to lick him, bottle him, anything to have more of it.

And he's even more gorgeous than I remembered. The gold-streaked hair, the pale blue eyes, and a body that was made for sex—lean enough to be mobile and built enough to feel like sin under my palms. He's wearing a pair of perfectly worn jeans, that t-shirt of his, and a now-open flannel. I'm a sucker for that not-quite-a-cowboy, not-quite-a-preppie look.

Mmm.

So.

I have this small problem.

Pregnancy has made me exceptionally, obsessively, insatiably horny.

"Marigold?" he asks. Does he sense my untethered lust?

"Call me Mari," I say, snapping myself back to the moment at hand.

"Look," he says. "I'm sorry I got you in this situation."

"*We* got me in this situation," I correct.

"I should have used a condom." He winces. "Sorry," he says, aiming the word right at my belly, as if he's apologizing directly to the baby for negating it. "I didn't mean it the way it sounded. I just meant, I didn't do the responsible thing that night. And I'd like to. Now. I'm here, and I can help with this. We can do it together, whatever you need."

My insides are jumping around, and not just because there's a teeny person hanging out in there, although the baby is kicking like a Rockette. I don't know what to think or feel. Part of me is so hugely relieved, I can't even breathe.

The other half of me is scared out of my mind. Until now, I knew what my options were, even if I didn't love them.

Now? Things are much more complicated. Legally, Kane could prevent me from arranging an adoption. I gave him that power when I told him he was the dad, when I decided to be totally honest with him.

He could want to raise the baby himself.

And I have no idea, yet, how to feel about that possibility.

Before I came to Rush Creek, I called several references to see if the Wilders were decent people to work for, and no one had anything but glowing praise about the family or the business. Unless Kane is secretly an evil seed, I think I'm probably safe.

Still. Fundamentally, I don't know this guy from Adam. The only thing that connects us is the fact that our DNA is all intertwined and growing a person in my lower abdomen.

Okay, maybe that's not an "only" kind of thing.

And also, maybe it's not our only connection. Maybe one night of insane sex isn't the same as years of getting-to-know-you, but it is a connection.

Like the kind a power cord makes with an outlet.

Regardless, there's no going back. No matter what the nature of our connection is—or will become—I'm not planning to start it off with any kind of deception or dishonesty, which means I have to lay my own stuff on the table.

"Um," I say. "Here's the thing. I was..."

My turn to wince.

"Before this, before I chanced on finding you—I was planning to choose adoption."

6

KANE

I wasn't expecting that, and I know my face shows it, as much as I try to hide my reaction. I manage, somehow, not to let any words out of my mouth, like, "Hell no!" Or, "I don't think that baby's Aunt Amanda, not to mention Grandma Barb, are going to like that idea." After all, this is the twenty-first century, I am reasonably enlightened, and that baby is growing inside her body, not mine—not to mention the fact that I know women generally end up doing a lot more of the childcare than men.

I also know a weirdly above-average amount about Oregon parental consent laws, because my brother Brody's path to fathering Justin was... unusual. So, for example, I know that my consent would be needed in order for her to arrange an adoption.

I don't say that out loud. There's too much I need to know before I can start throwing my weight around by citing laws and insisting on rights.

I ask, "Is it already set up? The adoption?"

She shakes her head. "That's the thing. I guess I wasn't as sure as I needed to be. I've been... procrastinating."

She's so sheepish that I have to hold back a smile. OK, so it's not a done deal.

And suddenly I feel weirdly calm. And certain.

I *want* this baby.

I even want us to raise it together.

I tell myself that this idea of mine, this *together* idea, has nothing to do with how the sight of those white teeth worrying the plump flesh of her lip affects me. This is about what's best for the baby—and maybe also my whole family, because they're going to go nuts with joy when they hear about another Wilder kid.

I mean, once they get over the whole thing about how I got a woman pregnant in a hotel lobby bathroom in Vegas.

Guess the boy next door has *truly* left the room.

I'm now a guy who knocked up a woman by way of a one-night stand.

The thought, improbably, makes me smile.

She notices. "You're smiling."

"Uh. Long thought-train."

"No, I mean, smiling's better than the alternative. I didn't know if I'd ever track you down, and I didn't know how you'd react when I did. I mean, some guys—"

"I'm not some guys."

She raises an eyebrow, and a dimple appears in her cheek. "No," she says. "You're definitely not."

Before I can respond to the tease in her voice—or even fully assimilate it—there's at least one compliment in there —she says, "I'm glad you're not being an asshole about it."

"Well, me too," I say. "Because I don't think I could live with myself if I were."

She cocks her head, eyebrows drawing together. "You're different than I remembered."

I shrug. It doesn't feel like now's the time to get into it—how I was channeling my brother Easton, how pretty much everything I did that night was out of character for me. "It was a while ago, and things happened quickly."

She squints at me, and I feel like she's not totally satisfied with that answer, but she doesn't call me out.

Quickly, I say, "So tell me where things stand. With the adoption possibility."

She quickly outlines the situation: a lot of time spent reading adoption profiles and four missed appointments with an adoption counselor. "I need to make a decision soon."

"You said you weren't sure that you want to—" I search for the right words. Brody had told me it's not cool to say 'give the baby up.' What about "—do an adoption?" Okay, that's a little awkward, too, but I'm still figuring this shit out.

A quick movement draws my eyes to where she clutches her wrist with one hand. At first, I think she's hurt, but then I realize she's twirling a shiny silver bracelet, round and round; it's a nervous tick.

"I thought I wanted adoption. I didn't think... correction, I *don't* think I'm mom material. My childhood situation—" She hesitates. "It was just my mom and me growing up. And she left when I was thirteen. For good."

"I'm sorry."

She waves it off. "My aunt was good to me. I mean, she

was pretty busy with my cousins, but she took good care of me. It's not like I was in foster care, or abused, or anything."

I try to imagine being in her shoes, but that lands me about as far as I can imagine from the pile-of-puppies family love I grew up with. Well, at least until my dad died. I want to hug her—and tell her that even if your childhood wasn't the suckiest thing that could happen to someone, it's okay to feel sad about it.

Before I can move or speak, she jumps in again. "My mom didn't have a nurturing bone in her body, and I have no reason to think I'd be any different. I'm just like her in a lot of ways. Neither of us knows how to stay put. I've been on the road my whole life, and I can't imagine wanting it otherwise. And that's not the right way for a kid to grow up."

I can't imagine wanting it otherwise.

Well, shit. That doesn't sound like someone who's just been waiting for me to make a marriage offer before changing her mind about an adoption.

And yet...

I would never try to get someone to do something they didn't want to do. I know when someone tells you who they are, you're supposed to believe them. And Mari has just told me she doesn't feel like she can mother a child.

But maybe, if she weren't in it alone?

"Give this three weeks." The words are out of my mouth before I can shape them or smooth them.

She stares at me.

"Stay here, design the trailers, help us spec the reno. Let you and me work out what we want to do. Together."

"Together," she repeats, sounding pained.

I realize immediately how it sounds, and regroup. "Decide together, I mean. About what makes the most sense for the baby. I could—" I hesitate, not wanting to scare her again, but also wanting to lay out the options. "I could do it. Raise it. And if I did, my family would be behind me a hundred percent."

She's thinking about it. Biting her lip. She doesn't hate the idea, I can tell. My chest fills with something. Excitement. Hope.

I dig in harder. "Give me a chance to make you fall in love with Rush Creek. With my family."

With me.

No, Kane, I chide myself.

That night in Vegas messed me up. No doubt. I'd never had sex like that, in-your-head, under-your-skin, smacked-in-your-chest sex.

But it was still just sex. I have to put it aside for the bigger good here. My baby's future. My family's chance to have a relationship with the kid.

This isn't about me, or how she feels about me, or how much I want to…

Nope. Just no.

No matter how good it felt to make her beg.

I banish the memories to the brain-porn dungeon and hammer my point home.

"Take some time, figure out what it would mean to let the baby grow up in Rush Creek. Give the idea of staying here a chance."

Now her mouth is hanging open.

"I—" She closes it. "Kane. That's—that last part. I don't

want to lie to you. I can't imagine myself wanting to settle down. I told you how I felt about staying put."

If I were Gabe, or Clark, or even Brody, I'd push. I'd haul out the big male energy and fight back. I'd tell her why she has to stay, why it's the only right way.

I might even use sex to do it.

But I'm not Gabe or Clark or Brody.

For better or worse, I'm me.

"I hear you," I say. "And if you can't do this, I understand." I say it with so much conviction, I almost believe it. That it doesn't matter to me whether she stays or goes. "But if you're thinking of choosing adoption..."

I reach out to touch her hand where she's fidgeting with her bracelet.

"Then please give me the chance to convince you to let me and my family raise the baby instead."

7

MARI

It's what I've wished for all these months.

If I'm completely honest with myself, it's why I canceled those appointments, why I never let myself fall in love with any of the family profiles I read.

Because part of me hoped against hope that I would find the baby's dad and he would say all the right things.

Just like Kane has.

And yet—

As much as it's a relief, it's also scary.

Because now that I'm face to face with this situation, I realize: I don't know this guy.

He caught you when you fell.

He's been nothing but civilized about this conversation, even though you showed up out of the blue and totally blindsided him with your giant belly. Even though we both know he could be on the phone with lawyers right this second.

He fucks like a dream.

Oh, Jesus, pregnancy hormones, *shut up!*

But fundamentally, I don't know him. I don't know who

he is or whether he's responsible. I don't know if he's a good guy or an asshole or even a criminal.

His eyes are lit up, his face animated. "You're going to love my family, Mari. My brothers can be a little... over the top when you first meet them. But their wives and girlfriends are incredibly supportive. My sister is a force to be reckoned with, in the best possible way. My mom is one of the most nurturing people I know. Well, duh, she's my mom, but still. Her partner, Geneva, is great, too. And Rush Creek is a sweet place to grow up. Yeah, it can be a little gossipy. But it's supportive. Neighbors helping neighbors. Someone gets sick, everyone brings food."

Even if that's not my thing, it still sounds awfully nice.

I remember being on the road with my mom, how one time we both got the flu. We were so sick, neither of us could get out of bed. I was so scared. What if something happened to my mom? Who would help?

No one. It was just us.

And then it was just me.

I want the baby to have the safety net I never did.

He must see me wavering.

"I know this must feel like a lot. Take your time. Don't say anything. Just, let me show you what it could be like," he says.

"For the baby?"

He hesitates. "For the baby, yeah," he says. "And for you, too. At least give me a chance to show you how I take care of someone. Park your Airstream on my property. I'll cook you breakfasts. And I make a mean hot breakfast."

I can't help it: I moan. Breakfast is my favorite meal, and

I was never morning-sick, so I've been eating for two since even before I knew we *were* two.

The corner of his mouth quirks up. "That's a good moan, right?" he asks. "I'll throw in foot massages, too."

There's a tease in his voice now, and God, he has *no* idea how tempting both those things are. He's just kidding, but my whole body started tingling at the thought of his big hands on my perpetually sore feet.

I can picture it vividly, and his hands don't stay on my feet in the fantasy. Slightly calloused against the smooth skin of my thighs, those hands slide up my legs...

Mari! Focus!

I don't want to give him false hope. That I could make motherhood, or family life, work.

Or maybe I don't want to give myself false hope. That I could be a person who settles down. In a small town. As a mother.

That despite my genes, I have it in me.

I twist my bracelet. It's a thing I do. My mom gave me this bracelet for my thirteenth birthday—which was the last one we celebrated together where we were both in the same place. "Look..." I start, but even before I can speak, he holds up a hand.

"I'm sorry," he says. "Too much?"

Relieved, I nod. "Too much. I mean, maybe not the RV parking."

He smiles.

"I appreciate that. But the rest—"

"Backing off," he says, both hands up now. He even takes a step backwards, a literal step, which makes me smile, a little.

The smile slides off my face as I think of something else. "What about your family? I know you said they're great, but in reality, are they going to freak out the second they know the baby is yours?"

Raking a hand through his hair and frowning, he ponders that. "Maybe we don't tell them yet. Give both of us a little time to think, huh?"

"I know I'm asking you to keep a pretty big secret from them."

He rolls his eyes. "My mom was with Geneva for months before she went public. Clark was fake dating his girlfriend, Jessa, for weeks before he told us it wasn't real. Brody had this complicated situation with his son, and none of us knew. Even Gabe slept with Lucy plenty of times before he let on they were seeing each other. So it's my turn. It's only fair, really. You don't want to tell them right away? We won't tell them right away."

Even though I asked, I'm startled he agreed. "Really?"

"Really. Well, except Clark," he says, frowning. "That boat left the dock. He was the only one I told about Vegas, so when he saw you—"

His eyes drop to my belly, and there's a softness in them that makes my chest hurt.

"Yeah," he says. "Clark knows the score. But I won't tell anyone else, and I'll tell Clark not to let on to any of them."

"Do you think he'll—?"

"I know he'll keep the secret if I ask him to. He's a vault."

Feeling a tightness in my chest, I take a deep breath. It might be the fear of giving up my freedom, the fear of losing control, or it might be something else. Excitement. Anticipation.

Hope.

I have to give this a chance. I know, and he knows, that he could have come on like a freight train about dads' rights and legal this, legal that, but all he's asked is for me to decide this *with him*.

After months of being terrifyingly alone, *with* is an awfully nice word.

Three weeks. That's all he's asking. And if I don't feel sure about him and his family by then—then I'll figure out what my options are.

"Okay," I say. "Three weeks."

8

———————

KANE

After I walk away from Mari—promising that we'll talk later and explaining to her how to find my house and the parking spot for her Airstream—I wander back to the office to fill in Clark.

I know he's in there, dying to know what the hell's going on. Even though Clark's my least gossipy brother, there is no way he's not tearing his hair out waiting for an update.

And sure enough, when I step through the flimsy trailer door, he's sitting in his cheap swivel desk chair, waiting for me. He immediately lunges out of the chair and grabs me by the arms. "Is it yours?"

I laugh, because the situation is so absurd, and his agitation is so extreme, and I need to blow off steam.

He looks at me like I've lost my mind, which maybe I have.

I sink into the guest chair. "Jesus, I need a beer."

He grabs two from the low-slung dorm fridge next to his desk, pops the tops, and hands me one. "I wish I had something stronger for you, dude."

I down a huge slug of beer, take a deep breath, and say, "It's mine."

"Are you *sure*?"

"Well, no, of course not," I say. "But she offered a paternity test, so I guess I'll do that. She said there's some noninvasive way they can test, but honestly, I believe her. If there were another guy who was easier to track down than me, wouldn't she have done that? It's not like she came here looking for anything. She had no idea I was here." I frown at Clark. "You didn't warn her?"

"When she showed up and I realized she was pregnant, I said 'I think you might know my brother.'"

"But not, 'I think my brother might be the father of your baby.'"

"Seriously?" he demands. "If I was wrong, that would have been so awkward."

"As opposed to what just happened out there, which was not-at-all awkward?"

We glare at each other, and then I start laughing again.

"Kane. You okay?"

"Sort of?" I sigh and take another slug of beer. "She'd been planning to choose adoption. Until she found me."

"Whoa," Clark says, big-eyed. "What did you say to that?"

"I asked her to take some time. Reconsider. Let me in on the decision-making process." I hesitate. I almost don't say it... but this is Clark. If anyone can understand where I'm coming from, it's him. "If she can't get her head around the idea of raising it maybe I could."

"Double whoa. That would be a fuck ton of work, Kane. Raising a kid?"

"I know how much work it would be. But it's what I want. You know I've always wanted kids."

"I know, but you wanted them in the context of marriage and a family, right? What about Veronica?"

"We broke up."

His eyes go wide. "You—when did that happen?"

I bring him up to date on the events of the morning. You'd think he'd be beyond surprise at the moment, but the breakup-by-parents still has shock power, and his mouth drops open.

"Wow. You've had quite the day. So Veronica's out of the picture... But are you sure you want to go down this path with Marigold?"

"I mean, what's the alternative? Tell her to go ahead, arrange the adoption? Let her and the baby walk out of my life?"

We stare at each other. He's the first to look away. When he looks back, he says, "I know how crazy you were about her. Marigold. I've never seen you the way you were after that one-nighter."

"Yeah."

Clark's the only one who knows how much that night rocked my world, how hard I worked, unsuccessfully, to get her out from under my skin.

He shakes his head. "This is nuts, Kane. It's so impulsive. It's not you."

"*Me* hasn't been working that well for me lately."

"What's that supposed to mean?"

"It means I'm tired of doing the safe thing. The sane thing. The well-trodden path. *If what you're doing isn't working, try anything else*," I quote. I finish the rest of the beer in a long continuous swig, and Clark hands me his, still untouched. He leans back toward the fridge to snag himself another one.

When he faces me again, eyes gentle on mine, he says, "I'll back your play, dude. You know that."

I'd guessed he'd be on my side no matter what, but still, hearing it feels good. "Thanks." The word feels inadequate. "I asked her to give me three weeks."

"To convince her to sign over rights?"

"Or to stay so we can raise the baby together."

His face darkens. "Kane. Are you *sure* you're thinking straight on this? Tell me this isn't just about her. About the sex."

"It's *not* about the sex," I say. "What matters is getting the baby's future sorted out, not me getting laid. I'm going to keep my hands to myself and my dick in my pants, till we figure this out."

He shakes his head. "If I had money for every Wilder brother who's uttered those words, or ones just like them, I wouldn't need to renovate those fucking trailers."

"This is hard core, though, Clark. Baby's *future*."

We both sit with that for a moment.

"What do you think the chances are? Of convincing her to stay?"

"I don't know. She's lived her whole life on the road and said she'd never thought about having it be different."

He squints. "Lucy didn't think she wanted small town life."

"Yeah, well, Lucy also didn't live in an Airstream motorhome and design RVs for a living."

"Point taken," he says. "On the other hand..." His mouth quirks. "Wilders are persuasive."

"They are that."

"So... what now?"

"Now I do everything I can to show her how amazing things could be. And that I'd make one hell of a dad."

Clark shrugs. "Piece of cake." He frowns. "But if you can't convince her? What if..." He frowns. "What if she flakes and leaves with the baby or something?"

"I'm not going to think about that now," I say. "Whatever happens, I'll deal with it. When I didn't put that condom on, I signed up to figure all of this out."

My brother's expression slowly eases. "You're a good man, Kane." He pulls out his phone. "You want me to call a family meeting? Lay this out for everyone? They'll all back your play. Amanda, Mom, all of them. That baby will have more aunties than it'll know what to do with. And uncles."

"Yeah, so about that," I say. "I definitely want her to see the Wilders in action. Maybe have Jessa invite her to a family dinner or something, so she can see how great everyone is with the kids. But you can't tell anyone yet that the baby's mine."

"Wait, *what*?"

I explain to him about Mari's legit worry that if everyone knows, they'll bear down on her.

"I think this is going to go better if she can just get to know me, get to know the family, get to trust us. Make up her mind. Then we can unleash the hounds of Wilder. The last thing I want is to scare her off by having Mom and Amanda try to talk her into anything."

Clark snickers. "Okay, you might have a point. That

said, there's no fucking way you're keeping this thing under wraps. She's, what—seven months pregnant? It's not subtle."

"Yeah, but you're the only one who knows I've ever seen her before today."

He opens, then closes, his mouth. "Wow. Yeah. Actually. You're right."

"She could have a husband and three other kids somewhere in Alabama. What would possibly make everyone think I got her pregnant?"

He leans back in his chair. "Huh. Yeah." His forehead wrinkles. "But you're a Wilder male, and this is Rush Creek, Kane, the gossip capital of the universe. This is where secrets come to walk like the undead. And you may think you're a superhero of make believe, but you probably aren't as good at hiding things from the women of this family as you think you are."

He fixes me with a laser sharp gaze.

"Take it from a guy who tried and failed."

9

MARI

K*nock.*

Knock knock.

No, it's not a joke.

Someone is knocking on Bernadette's door.

"Whah?" It's not even really a question. It's a grunt.

"Mari." It's Kane's voice. "I made breakfast."

I groan. I am so not a morning person. I can't even lift my head off the pillow. I groan and try again. I'm slightly more successful this time. The baby kicks my bladder, and suddenly I'm wide awake. Yep, I'll be getting up now.

"It's an avocado, bacon, cheese, and tomato omelet."

"Oh, wow," I say.

I slowly haul myself off the bed. My hips grouse. My back creaks. I imagine this is how old women feel. Minus the creature turning somersaults in my abdomen.

I drag myself into the bathroom and catch sight of myself in the mirror. My hair is a wild tangle, there's dried drool on my cheek, and my eyes have huge circles under them. Damn. I start trying to get myself presentable, then quit, because, well, it's hopeless. Instead, I yank my hair into the messiest messy bun on earth and open the door to find him standing there, wearing a dark green sweater over a pair of well-worn jeans. He's freshly showered and recently shaved and grinning at me.

I cross my arms as casually as I can over my rapidly hardening nipples. Can't blame it on the cold, although in fairness, it's got to be barely thirty out there.

"I thought we agreed you weren't going to cook for me," I say, as a defense against everything I want to do right now, namely, grab him and rub myself all over him.

His grin subsides, but doesn't disappear completely, one corner of his mouth lifting higher than the other as he shrugs. "It's not for you. It's for the baby."

If I'm a little disappointed, I quickly remind myself that it's for the best. Not getting anyone's hopes up about the possibility of a happy little family. "Gotcha."

"Come on up when you're ready?"

"To your house?"

He raises an eyebrow. "Unless you want me to bring it here?"

"No—no, that's okay," I say, even though it would probably be safer for me to hide in here and eat by myself. But if there's a chance Kane's going to raise the baby, I should know what the inside of his house looks like. How he lives. If he's neat, if he's clean, if there are live mousetraps or loose floorboards or, I don't know, copies of *Serial Killer How-To Quarterly* magazine lying around. Anyway, I should scope out Kane's living situation to get a clear picture of his suitability as a parent. Or so I tell myself. "Give me a few minutes."

When he's gone, I change quickly into presentable clothes. Then I head up to the house.

Last night, I followed Kane's directions and parked Bernadette in a clearing next to his driveway, beside what looks like a toolshed. In the light of morning, I can see that we're fully hidden in the woods—just Bernadette, the shed, and the house are visible. Otherwise, it's all trees.

From the outside, the house is tiny but adorable, a log cabin like you'd see in a book, with a small porch in front. There's a woodpile against one outside wall, along with an axe, a maul, and a smaller heap of split wood. And smoke rises from what must be a woodstove inside. Although the whole thing is surrounded by tall evergreens, the clearing around the house is just large enough for light to dapple it from above.

It feels like a secret. If I ever *were* to settle down, I would want it to be somewhere like this, away from crowds and prying eyes.

I knock at Kane's dark green front door, and he opens it, stepping back to let me in.

"Oh!" I say, glancing around. "This is so cool!"

I've stepped into a single "great room."

Everything's white, a fresh, bright white—the logs that make up the walls, the beams of the ceiling, and all the other exposed wood. There's a pale stone fireplace, a gray couch and matching chair, a big light-wood dining room table, and a small but modern kitchen, where two steaming plates of breakfast sit on a central island.

"I love the white paint on the logs!"

"Yeah, me too. My realtor friend said not to do it for

resale reasons, but I like the way it turned out." He gestures. "Come. Sit."

I follow his instruction, my mouth falling open when I see the food up close. "Oh my God, Kane, this is *amazing*. It's like a restaurant. Fruit? Toast? OJ?"

He shrugs and sits beside me. "Breakfast is my favorite meal. Dig in."

He doesn't have to ask me twice. It tastes as good as it looks, and I mostly suppress a moan of pleasure at the perfectly crispy bacon, ripe avocado, Jack cheese, and fresh tomato, all in the perfect proportions. Not to mention *fresh-squeezed orange juice.*

"Were you up at dawn squeezing oranges?" I demand. "Who *are* you? If you'd told me in Vegas that you had other talents, I might have insisted on getting your name."

He grins at that. "*Other* talents?" He quirks an eyebrow.

Whoops. I can feel my face going hot. "Not gonna lie," I tell him, with a nonchalant shrug—or the best I can manage. "It was memorable."

His eyes flash, and suddenly I can see the other man, the one who locked the door of the hotel lounge-style bathroom and stalked me across the carpet. "Glad to hear it."

My gaze drops from his dark eyes to the softness of his lower lip.

That mouth. I didn't get a chance to find out everything it could do...

He breaks the eye contact, picks up his fork, and resumes eating.

Right.

Just because I'm pregnant and the increased blood flow to my sexual organs is robbing my brain of good sense, doesn't mean that the same thing is happening to him.

Do. Not. Think. About. The. Blood. Flow. To. Kane's. Sex. Organs.

Kane politely coughs. "Tell me more about where things stand with the adoption situation," he says, and my gaze flicks to his face. I suspect he's also trying to get us back to sensible territory.

Does that mean he took a detour from it with me? Was he also thinking lovely, dirty things?

It shouldn't matter.

Much.

I shake myself internally. "Yeah, so, I've read about a million family profiles."

"Did you find ones you liked?"

"There were a lot of good ones."

"What makes one good?"

I remember thinking, in Vegas, that Kane asked interesting questions. Not small talk questions. If he'd asked small talk questions, maybe he would have known what I did for a living, or that I lived in an Airstream, or that my whole life had been itinerant—and maybe I'd have known that he was a Wilder brother and led ski trips in Oregon. Instead, he asked things like, *What was the last movie you watched that you loved?* and then we went down this huge rabbit hole talking about *Dune* until both of us were lit up about movie adaptations and books that change your life and probably a lot of misplaced, redirected lust for Timothée Chalamet and Zendaya. Although in all fairness, I wasn't thinking of Timothée Chalamet at *all* when I propositioned Kane. I was lost in the pull between us, so strong that I felt like I'd die if I didn't kiss him, if I couldn't feel his big hands—gesturing to make a point about the beauty of the desert sand and those spice-blue eyes—on my skin.

Maybe you don't have to know anything at all about someone to know who they are.

"Mari?" he asks.

"Sorry," I say. "I went—somewhere else."

He looks like he wants to ask more, but just then his phone buzzes.

"It's Clark," he says. "Gotta take it." He steps out of the great room area, toward what I assume is a bedroom, and I can hear him talking to his brother.

I get up from the counter and cross to the far wall, which is covered with photographs, matted with white and framed in black. I can tell many of them are Wilder family members—the resemblance is strong—but a few are unfamiliar faces or landscapes. They're all incredibly striking and distinctive.

Footsteps approach behind me.

"These are—" I turn to look at him. "These are *amazing*, Kane. I mean, look at her expression." I gesture at a photo of Amanda. "Is this your sister?"

"Mmm-hmm. And her daughter, Anna."

The girl, who'd I guess is ten or so, is serving soup from an industrial-sized tureen to a man in a torn greatcoat and battered top hat. Amanda stands slightly behind her, just barely in focus. It's the look on Amanda's face that's so arresting: pride and soft delight. It makes something feel loose and warm in the center of my chest.

"That was at the Rush Creek Food Pantry," he says.

He's caught his sister in such a moment of vulnerability

and love. And I haven't met Amanda, but I can't imagine she lets herself have many of those moments in public. Kane must have been looking for it.

He saw it and captured it.

"And this one?" I point to a photo of Clark. He's holding a toddler, and his face is turned away—but Kane has managed to capture just enough that you can see the pain etched across it. He's—wrecked. "What—what happened to him?"

Kane's eyes shutter. "That was just a few months after his wife died. This was before he met Jessa. It was a hard time for him. That's Amanda's youngest, Kieran, in his arms."

"God."

I want to reach out to touch it, to smooth the lines of grief and agony. That's how real and present it feels.

"Have you done anything with these? Shown them anywhere?"

"Nah," he says, shrugging it off. "They're just for me."

"Maybe they shouldn't be," I suggest. "I've been around this country a lot, seen a lot of art shows and galleries... and these aren't just good. They're *good* good."

He shrugs again. "Thanks. I really appreciate it. But—yeah, it's just a hobby."

"Kane, you're—" Doesn't he know? "I don't think you understand how beautiful these are. You capture so much emotion. It comes across so strongly. These are *art*."

"Thank you," he says.

His gaze drops, and I follow it with my own. Sometime during my speech, I must have impulsively reached out to put my hand on his arm. My fingers are wrapped over the thickest part of his forearm. Even through his sweater, he's like a furnace. The heat of his skin travels up my own arm and makes my ever-ready nipples tingle.

I yank my hand back.

"Dishes. Let me help you with the dishes."

If he's confused by the sudden change of topic, he doesn't show it.

10

KANE

"You have a minute?" Gabe asks me.

"Sure."

"Hanna?" Gabe calls.

Hanna is bent over a pair of skis, examining the binding. In this snowless ski season, we've checked and rechecked the equipment so many times—for lack of something more useful to do—that I have its contours memorized. I'm sure there's nothing new to see—but I know she's as bored as I am, so I don't begrudge it.

She raises her head. "Yeah?"

"Lucy and I need a few minutes with you and Kane."

Those words, as innocuous as they sound, strike fear in my heart. When Gabe and Lucy want to talk to anyone in the business, it means they've been strategizing, and when they've been strategizing, change is always afoot.

I hate change.

Or, well, I used to think I did. I've spent a lot of years hating change, because change is when your dad dies, your mom gets cancer, and your big brother turns into a tyrant, all in the space of a year.

But maybe change is also what happens when you do something totally out of character—and it shows up on your doorstep seven months later.

And that kind of change... doesn't feel all bad.

It feels good, like watching Mari eat the breakfast I'd cooked.

Like listening as she told me that my photographs were beautiful. That they were art.

Like soaking up the sensation of her hand on my arm.

Spending time with her makes me want to spend more. It makes me think about what else I can do to convince her to give me a chance—not just as a dad, but... well, as a man.

Breakfast was a good start, but obviously it's not enough.

"Kane," Gabe says sharply. I've wandered off in my head, and he's looking at me strangely.

"Here!" I return, soldier-voiced, resisting the temptation to salute. Gabe doesn't always have a sense of humor about his bossiness.

The four of us—Hanna, Lucy, Gabe, and I—sit at the central table, and Gabe leans forward.

"We're leaning toward phasing out ski trips."

I choke on my own saliva.

Gabe eyes me. "They're not bringing in money.

"It hasn't *snowed*." There's an unusual edge in my voice.

He rolls his eyes at me. "Over the last five years, this year excluded for obvious reasons, the share of revenue from ski trips has dropped precipitously."

Lucy, who is not just a brilliant marketer but also a

diplomat, jumps in. "We're not phasing out winter trips. In fact, we want to make winter an even bigger part of our strategy. We think people are hungry for winter activities, and there are more winter weddings now than ever, not to mention people who want to use the hot springs in the cold months. So we want your input on a few things. We're looking at introducing igloo camping—"

"Igloo camping?" Hanna is not just a family friend and my business partner but the absolute uncontested master of scorn, and when she turns it on full volume, it is *scathing*.

"Glass igloos," Lucy confirms, apparently unscathed. "We're looking at the success of glamping and see that we need to up our game, not just with the Airstreams and Clark's Gilderness trips, but across the board. The snow-shoe-and-cocoa trips were wildly successful last winter, so we'd like to do more of those whenever it snows again, but we're also thinking they could be expanded into overnights."

She smiles warmly at us. "We want input from both of you. Not immediately, but we'd like to meet again in a couple of weeks and do some brainstorming about where you see your winter business going."

Hanna and I exchange glances.

"I know it's a lot," Lucy says.

"They can handle it," Gabe says. "Right, guys?"

Hanna nods. "Right."

I don't say anything because I'm afraid of what will come out.

"So," Gabe says, turning to me abruptly. "Are the rumors true?"

My mouth falls open. "What?!" Clark *promised* he wouldn't tell.

"Rumor has it there's a pregnant RV designer living in her Airstream on your land. Scandalous."

I wheeze in a breath, trying not to make it too obvious that I was holding it. "Oh, right. Yeah. She needed a place to park the RV, and that made the most sense."

Lucy smiles. "That was nice of you."

"Uh, yeah, thanks."

"Jessa thinks we should invite her to family dinner next weekend."

"Yes!"

They all turn to look at me. I dial down the intensity and try again. "I bet she'd enjoy that. I mean, who doesn't love a Wilder party, right?"

Hanna is squinting at me. "Kane, do you have a *crush* on her?"

Whoops.

But it's better than the alternative, right? There are other questions she could have asked that would have been way worse.

Like, *Is that your bun in her oven?*

Why, yes, yes, it is, funny you should ask.

"No. Nope. No crush."

Now all three of them are staring at me. "She's pregnant," I say. "There's gotta be a dad in the picture somewhere." It's a hundred percent the truth, while also being a terrible lie of omission.

"Clark says she's single."

"Still. She's pregnant, so it's complicated."

"Yeah, well." Gabe shrugs. "No Wilder brother ever does anything the easy way."

"Very true." Lucy beams at him and reaches for his hand. They exchange lovey glances.

Neither of them has the slightest idea *how* true it is in my case, and I'd like to keep it that way.

"You want to head to the house and grab some lunch?" Gabe asks Lucy.

I roll my eyes. Everyone at Wilder knows what that's code for. On the plus side, they've completely forgotten about me.

When I look up, though, Hanna is eyeing me curiously.

I cross my arms. "I *don't* have a crush on her."

"Okay, boss." She shrugs. "Whatever you say."

11

MARI

On the second morning, Kane knocks around the same time, and when I groan in response—definitely nothing that remotely resembles words—he calls out, "Can I come in? I brought your breakfast. It's hot."

My stomach growls, loud enough that it's possible he can hear it. He brought me breakfast *in bed*. How is this my life?

He'll feed the baby well, I tell myself. That's why the thought of a hot breakfast in Kane's hands makes me feel like crying. That, and pregnancy hormones.

Blame everything on the pregnancy hormones.

"Come in," I call.

I drag myself to sitting, wishing I didn't look like something the cat barfed up. Or maybe I should be glad I do. Because it keeps things simple, knowing I'm not desirable in my current state.

If I felt like I was in a position to seduce Kane, I'd be so tempted to do it.

He's kind of a dream.

Every *other* woman's dream, that is. It's unfair for him that he managed to knock up the type of woman who is impervious to domestic comforts. The type of woman who doesn't fantasize about a little picket-fenced cottage and breakfast in bed and two-point-five children running around the backyard.

Bernadette's door scrapes open, and Kane appears, tray in hands.

"Hey," he says. "I have to leave early for work, so I figured I'd bring this to you so you didn't have to get up till the last possible moment. You're clearly not a morning person."

"It's that obvious?"

He laughs. "Just a little." He looks around at the inside of my Airstream, in all her pink and white glory, and I realize I haven't introduced him.

"This is Bernadette." I gesture around us.

"Berna—?"

"That's her name," I say.

He tilts his head to one side. "She has a name."

"Of course she has a name."

"Does the baby have a name?"

That stops me cold. "No," I whisper.

I've never let myself refer to the baby as *my baby* and I've never given it a name. I've never even thought of it as a *he, she,* or *they* instead of an *it*. I don't know its sex—and that's for a reason.

I didn't want to make it any harder to say goodbye.

Kane makes a small sound of distress. "God, that was an asshole question," he says. "I'm really sorry."

"No, it's okay," I say. "Don't worry about it. You were just asking."

His forehead is creased, his mouth pinched. He feels really bad, obviously.

"So. Bernadette," he says, tearing his worried glance from my face to look around. "She's very... pink."

"Ha. Yes. She is."

Bernadette is all pink and white inside. Pink and white lino on the floor, pink and white striped cabinets in the kitchen. A pink range, a pink microwave, a pink table, pink bench seats. Pink gingham on the windows and the bedspread.

I even installed bookshelves with all pink books—which isn't as hard to do as it sounds. There are a lot of *great* pink books in the world, including a first edition hardcover of Carol Ryrie Brink's *The Pink Motel*, left over from my mother's childhood.

"Do you ever get—sick of it?"

I shake my head. "Not yet. At some point I'll get sick of it, tear it all out, and start over, but I wanted something distinctive. Something that would showcase my abilities."

"She does," he says. And then, seeming to grasp that he's being somewhat rude, "And I do really like Bernadette. I didn't mean I didn't."

"Really?"

"Yeah. She's super cute."

I explain that she needs a ton of work. "You know the thing about how the shoemaker's children never have shoes? That's Bernadette. She needs a new electrical system and to be re-water-tighted, and that's just the non-drive-train stuff—she's a mess."

"Well, she's a beautiful mess," he says, smiling at me.

I bite my lip.

He seems to suddenly recall why he's here and leans down to set the tray on the part of my lap that's still baby-free. It's steel cut oats drenched in butter, brown sugar, raisins, and slivered almonds; a plate of berries; and another glass of that ridiculous orange juice.

And even over the mouth-watering scents of butter and sugar and orange juice, I can smell his soap and deodorant and after-shave.

My stomach rumbles, loudly, but luckily the other hungry parts of me admire him without making any noise. I need to watch myself, or I'll end up grabbing his arm when I'm not paying attention, like I did yesterday morning. Or worse. I might grab something else.

He's still leaning over me, removing the plastic wrap from each topping. I could reach up and pull him down to me.

My mouth waters and my fingers itch. I can almost feel the softness of his hair under my fingertips—I remember that softness. But just as my willpower threatens to fail, he crumples the plastic wrap and steps back.

I huff out a breath of frustration and relief.

"I have to get to work, but just leave the plate in my sink when you're done," he instructs. "The door's always unlocked."

"You're a saint, Kane," I tell him.

The corner of his mouth turns up. "Hardly," he says dryly. "If I were a saint, you wouldn't be pregnant."

Our eyes meet.

He was definitely not a saint that night. And I didn't want him to be.

We're still staring at each other. His eyes are dark and hungry, and I want him to take a step towards me. Instead, his gaze slides away and he fidgets with the plastic wrap ball. "I should go. Bon appétit."

"Thank you."

As the door creaks shut behind him, *I* feel a tiny bit like a saint—for not eating him for breakfast.

12

MARI

The trailers Clark's first contractor spec'd out are *yaaaawwwwwn.*

They're luxurious, sure, but they look like they were cookie-cuttered out of beige and gray dough, like tiny corporate hotel rooms nestled inside Airstreams.

"Is this what you want? More of these?" I try to keep my voice neutral as he shows me the other guy's plan and materials for the remaining trailers—carpet squares, fabric samples, tile.

Clark's no dummy, though. He narrows his eyes at me. "It's what we thought we wanted. Why?"

"They're—" I hesitate. "Can I be honest?"

"Please," he says.

"They're bland. Vanilla pudding."

Clark's eyebrows rise practically to his hairline. "So, you've got a better idea?"

"I think I might. Show me the ones that aren't done yet."

"We don't have time to fuck around," Clark warns.

"I know."

He gives me a level look, which I return. I've designed trailers for a lot of men who think they know everything, and Clark, who's obviously a teddy bear, doesn't scare me at all.

"Don't make me regret giving you some rope," he says.

I smile. "I won't."

He takes me to the six trailers that are still waiting to be worked on. I reach into my satchel and pull out a clipboard and a tape measure, then begin making sketches and writing notes. I carefully determine specific dimensions. The good news is there's a lot to work with. Two of the trailers will have to be torn down to the bones, but the rest won't.

Taking my measurements along with some warnings from Clark, I drive Bernadette back to Kane's. I sit at my dinette with my laptop, sipping my favorite ginger tea, and work on a proposal.

Clark wants me to present my ideas to the entire Wilder Adventures crew next week. I don't like to leave anything to chance when I'm working on a project. And in this case, because I'm proposing something different from what Clark thought he wanted, I know I need to provide a near-perfect proposal.

I start by pulling together a Pinterest board to represent each of the trailers I'm envisioning.

This is one of my favorite parts of the job, and I pass a pleasant couple of hours filling my boards with photos.

When I'm done with that, I'll draft PowerPoint slides explaining my concept and showing some examples, and by the end of the weekend, I'll have filled pages of my sketchbook with detailed drawings.

Which reminds me: I need to take a closer look at the Wilder Adventures website and social media marketing. I need to make sure I'm lining up my proposal with Lucy's vision, which—Clark explained—is what has driven Wilder's current strategy.

Luckily for me, Lucy is obviously great at what she does, and the Wilder brand is crystal clear. I start jotting down words and phrases that jump out at me: "connection," "camaraderie," "self-discovery." "Making outdoor adventure fun, playful, and accessible." "The wilderness is the playground where you'll journey with your friends, discover your true self, and meet your new soulmates."

I want Lucy to write *my* marketing materials.

I hear a thud outside, then another, and manage to ignore them. But after ten minutes or so, when the thuds don't stop, curiosity gets the better of me. I need to stretch my legs anyway, so I step out of Bernadette and come face-to-face with a lovely sight: Kane Wilder, shirtless to the waist, splitting wood. His back is to me, gorgeous twin grooves on either side of his spine, muscle bunching and flexing in his shoulders. He raises the maul, letting me see his forearms at work, then brings it down.

Gahhhh.

How long is too long to stand, watching a man split wood? At what point does it cross over from, *I just stepped outside...* to *I am caught in a thirst trap, unable to move* territory?

The universe answers this question when Kane turns suddenly, maul still in his hands, and catches me watching.

His eyebrows go up.

I can feel my cheeks turn pink.

"I didn't realize I had an audience," he says, one corner of his mouth tilting.

"I just—" It's impossible to exonerate myself, but I give it my best shot. "I was just going to thank you again for the breakfasts."

He's brought me breakfast in bed every day.

"It's my pleasure." His smile grows, crinkles forming at the corners of his eyes. "Besides, I'm trying to sell my nurturing traits, and breakfast's what I've got."

"It's impressive," I say. "The waffles were fantastic."

We stand there awkwardly for a moment.

He sets the maul down. (*No! Don't let me stop you!*) "I've got to go into town for groceries. Can I get you anything?"

"No, I—I went yesterday."

He raises an eyebrow. "Pickles? Ice cream?"

I laugh. "My cravings are so much weirder than that. Grapefruit. Canned peaches. Boston cream pie, and let me tell you, it is *not* so easy to get Boston cream pie around here."

He grins. "I bet we can find some. I love a good challenge." He tilts his head. "You busy? Want to go on a Boston cream pie hunt?"

"I was—"

My body's all discombobulated, my mouth watering at the thought of getting my craving fulfilled, my eyes unable to leave the gleam of sweat on Kane's sculpted torso. Boston cream pie. Kane Wilder. Two irresistible temptations.

Plus getting to know Rush Creek a little better *would*

help me create an even stronger presentation, and make sure my ideas are in line with the vibe of the town.

Win. Win. Win.

"Sure," I say, and am rewarded with white teeth, eye crinkles, and a dimple.

As if the taut pecs, thickly muscled shoulders, and six-pack abs were not enough to ruin me.

13

———

KANE

"First stop, Rush Creek Bakery. Our family friend Nan owns it. Ninety percent sure she doesn't have Boston cream pie, but she might have a recipe, or know who would."

Mari peers out the window as we drive up the main drag. "Oh, man, this place looks like a cowboy should amble out for a showdown in the middle of the street at any moment."

"It's been a while since that happened," I say dryly. "Clark told you about the transformation of Rush Creek?"

"That it was a hard-core rodeo town, and that the rodeo shut down basically the same day some hot spring popped up?"

"Yup, and now Rush Creek is a spa-and-wedding destination. Everything changed. It's like the town put on a party dress. Some people love it, some hate it—but it's different, for sure. Most of the businesses have adapted. The shopkeepers down here may not love the tourists, but they know which side their bread is buttered on."

She watches out the window. "Your tourists are mostly women, now, it looks like."

"Yup. Fewer cowboys, more middle-aged women, bevvies of bridesmaids, and couples."

I don't know why town's so crowded on a Monday in March, but the only open parking space is in front of Spa Day Sandwiches. I park and we exit the car, stepping onto the sidewalk.

"Wagon wheel, huh?" She wrinkles her nose at the giant one out front.

"It used to be Wagon Wheel Sandwiches."

"Ah. That makes more sense." She nods.

She follows me as I lead her toward Rush Creek Bakery, where I'm hoping Nan will be able to help with the Boston cream problem. We pass Oscar's Saloon and Grill, and I flash back to the night Clark and I drank too much whiskey and I confessed that I still wasn't over the pixie I'd fucked in Las Vegas. Now that pixie is standing next to me, pink-cheeked and round with my child—

My child.

It's the first time I've let myself think it, and *holy shit.*

I want to ask her how I'm doing at convincing her of my dad-worthiness, but it's still early—less than a week in— and she hasn't even met my family yet. A few breakfasts in bed can't have convinced her that I'd be a contender for Father of the Year.

She peeks in the window of Oscar's. "Saloon doors! Elk and moose heads! A mural!"

"I mean, you must have seen a hundred Western towns."

"Yes, and it *never* gets old. I love new places. Some

people would say that all Western towns look alike. I'd say each one is different." She eyes me sideways. "I bet you would, too. With that artist's eye. Different characters, different flavors."

I try not to let the artist's eye comment go to my head, because really, I don't have one. I just love taking pictures. "I don't travel much. Lots of family and business obligations. Tough to get away."

"Huh." I think she's going to say more, but she doesn't. And for a moment I regret my confession. Why would a woman who's seen so much want to be with a guy who's spent his life in one place?

But I'm not going to lie about who I am. I hope Mari knows that, and I hope she doesn't lie about who she is.

We pass Rush to Read Books, then a bunch of women's clothing and bridal shops.

"Feel free to check anything out if you're interested," I tell Mari.

"I'm guessing there's no maternity store."

I eye her belly, which definitely has an area code of its own at this point, and shake my head ruefully. "Nope."

"Anyway, I'm a Goodwill gal," she says. "Long habit. There's a Goodwill in most towns, it's always cheap, and I like picking out the stuff that's out of the mainstream."

That helps explain her wild garb—today she's wearing an orange tunic that looks almost woven, with stripes in different patterns, incorporating yellow, brown, and black.

"I like your clothes. They were one of the things that first made me notice you."

"Yeah?" she says, sounding pleased. "What were the others?"

We're walking side by side, not looking at each other, and maybe that's what makes me answer honestly. "Your hair."

I can see her, suddenly, in the bar, the dim light catching in the orange-and-gold of her wild mane. There might as well have been a spotlight on her.

"Yeah?" she says again, but it's different this time, almost provocative. It makes my pulse stutter.

Damn it, Kane, bad move.

Until just now, Vegas hadn't come up again since she teased me about my "talents" over breakfast that first morning. And it's probably a good thing, because thinking about that night has been kryptonite for me for months, and it definitely doesn't help the pact I made with myself to keep it in my pants.

And yet I don't seem to be able to stop myself. "The way you looked. Fierce, a little wild, but also... self-contained. Not like you were waiting for someone to pick you up. Like you were complete already."

Her breath hitches, like I've startled her.

"That's what I mean. You have an artist's way of seeing things. It makes me feel things." She gives a little laugh. "Not *sex* things, although those things, too. *Feelings* things."

That just makes it worse, because she's just outlined my exact problem: Mari lights me up on every channel. If it were just sex... well, it would be easier to tune out.

Luckily, we've arrived at our destination, and a subject change is easy—before I can get myself in any deeper.

"This is the place that I thought might be able to help us find Boston cream pie," I say, reaching for the handle on the door of the shop in front of us, Rush Creek Bakery.

We step in and are immediately greeted with the smell of fresh-baked bread. "Kane!" Nan calls out to me from behind the counter. She's tall and thin, and her fluffy gray hair is pulled up on her head. She's wearing a white apron, but it doesn't seem to have kept flour from getting everywhere, including the end of her nose. She comes out from behind the counter, hugs me, and says, "Oh, *my*, what have we *here*?"

"This is Mari. She's in town to help Clark refurbish his trailers."

Nan cocks her head. "So she's not Veronica's replacement?" She whispers it, but Nan's whispers can be heard across a football field.

I'd be shocked by the speed with which news travels, except that Nan and Sigrid are friends. "Nope," I tell her.

Nan's clearly disappointed. She's an honorary grandma to the Wilder kids, and I'm sure she's hoping for another one as soon as possible.

I don't tell her she's gonna get her wish. It would be all over town in twenty seconds. Nan is like the telephone operator of the old West: hub for all information in town.

"Nan, Mari has a craving for Boston cream pie. We were hoping you'd know where we could find her a piece."

"Well," she huffs. "It isn't *here*."

"No, I didn't think—"

"I don't do cakes," she reminds me sternly. "Or pies."

"No, I mean your breads and cookies are—"

"If an old-fashioned chocolate chip cookie isn't good enough for you—"

"Nan," I interrupt, because sometimes you have to manage Nan a bit. "We'll take two of your cookies. And a

loaf of French bread. Please. But this is a pregnancy crav-
ing-thing. It can't be argued with."

That seems to work, and Nan bustles about, getting us
our cookies and bread.

"Nan?" I call.

"Mmm-hmm?"

"Want me to take some photos for Facebook?"

She crosses her arms. "Hell, no."

"Just a couple."

She heaves an enormous sigh. "Sure."

I capture a few shots of her hands reaching into the
glass case, and a few of her expressions as she hands the
bags over the counter to Mari.

She scowls at both of us and waves me off as I try to pay.
"Send me those photos," she says grumpily. "And I hope
you aren't thinking of Carol's Cake Shop for that Boston
cream pie. Even if she could lower herself to make something as classic as *Boston cream pie*, it would probably be
vegan. Or gluten free."

There's nothing worse in Nan's book than gluten free.

"No. You're right. Carol's wouldn't be the place for it," I
soothe.

"You know where I'd try?" Nan tilts her head. "I'd try
the bakery at the feed store. They carry my cookies and
breads, so we know they're down to earth."

"Oh, good call," I tell her.

As soon as we're out of view of Nan's window, Mari
starts to laugh.

"Were you holding that in the whole time?" I ask, as we
start toward the feed store.

"A lot of it," she admits. "She's—fantastic."

"She's pretty excellent."

"So are these." I pull open the bag I'm carrying and hand her one of Nan's cookies. "Try this."

Mari takes a bite. "Oh. Ohhhhh."

Oh, hell. Mari moaning… is a problem for me.

"You, um—maybe shouldn't do that," I say, before I can stop myself.

"Do wha—oh." She bites her lip, then tilts her head, a teasing half-smile on her face. She's flirting. And shit, that's not helping. "Sorry. I won't do it again."

She takes another bite of cookie, pressing her lips together. "Better?"

I sigh.

No. Not better at all.

But way, way smarter.

We pass Morning Rush Coffee, the scent of dark roast thickening the air. "Hey," she says, nudging my shoulder with hers. "Who's Veronica?"

"Ex-girlfriend."

Her eyes are curious. "Recent?"

Is she maybe, just a tiny bit, *jealous*? I sneak a look, but her expression is neutral. Still, the possibility is way too appealing.

"We broke up recently, but it wasn't serious." This is an oversimplification, but it covers the necessary ground, especially since I've barely thought about Veronica in the last few days.

"So no heartbreak."

"No heartbreak," I agree.

I enjoy the fact that she sounds the tiniest bit relieved.

14

MARI

My heart pounds as I push through the swinging glass doors that front Wilder Adventures headquarters.

Today's the day I present my plan for the trailers. It's also the day I meet the baby's extended family—a big chunk of the Wilder crew.

And, except for Clark and Kane, they don't even know the newest Wilder is on board.

What could go wrong?

The Wilder headquarters is in a large barn. According to Clark, this land used to be a ranch, which makes sense. The barn apparently dates all the way back to those days. It's painted red, with a steep roof and just a few windows, but inside, it looks like an industrial-style open-plan office building—except with a loft over part of the big open main area.

People mill around a huge conference table in the center of the room, eating and chatting. I catch the scent of something that smells like lasagna. Yum. I'm early for my own presentation, because Clark said if I was, there'd be free lunch. I never turn down free lunch. And that's true times a thousand more since I've been pregnant.

I can't help it; my eyes search the room for Kane. He stands slightly to the side, taking photos on his phone. I wonder if his co-workers and family appreciate all the moments he captures for them.

Spinning through the Wilder social media yesterday, I could spot his photos right off; they're different from everyone else's. I recognized the way he frames people's faces, their expressions, and even their body language. In every photo, it's obvious how much he cares, how much he loves his friends and family, and how clearly he sees them.

As I approach the group of people, conversation stops, and eyes swing my way. Kane's big hands lower his phone, and I catch his glance long enough for a tingle to move through my blood. My heartbeat kicks up like it always does when his attention is on me. I think about what he said yesterday, how at the bar I looked *self-contained*. Like I was *complete already*.

That was how I'd felt in that moment. Alone but not lonely. Ready for something to happen, but not needing it to.

And then he'd walked over and blown my life wide open. Destroyed my self-containment, for better or for worse.

"Hey, everyone," Clark says, appearing at my shoulder. "This is our new RV designer, Mari Barrymore."

"Hi, Mari," says a tall man with a perfect dusting of stubble on his strong jaw. He's dark-haired, dark-eyed, and built like Clark, minus just a little of the over-the-top Viking physique. "I'm Gabe."

I shake Gabe's hand—he has a strong-but-not-bone-crushing-grip, which I appreciate. "Hi, Gabe."

"Gabe's the boss," Clark says.

Gabe's gaze drops to my belly, then rises. My heart rate kicks up again. I'm counting on the Wilders knowing that great Dave Barry advice: *Don't ever ask a woman if she's pregnant unless you see the baby coming out of her.*

Gabe has apparently heard that warning, because all he says is, "Welcome to Rush Creek. We're excited to hear the plan. In the meantime, grab some grub and meet the Wilders." He gestures to the small crowd of people and the table full of food—lasagna, salad, garlic bread.

Three women intercept me as I approach the table.

"I'm Lucy!" the first says. "Head of marketing and Gabe's wife. And the little one in the sling is Willow."

I'm not sure how Lucy's managed it, given the baby on her chest, but everything about her is perfect: hair, makeup, clothes. And yet she's not a classic queen bee-mean girl type, because she's smiling at me in an unmistakably friendly way and holding out a hand to shake.

"Lucy does most of Wilder's marketing and is the brains behind the rebranding. She'll be keeping tabs on our design decisions," Clark says, from behind me.

"In the nicest possible way." Lucy smiles warmly. Her gaze falls to my belly and climbs back to my face. She's curious, too, but she doesn't comment. Too well-mannered.

I start to think Dave Barry has my back, but then the second woman, who's sporting an awesome raven-haired pixie cut, points at my belly and says, "Are you *pregnant*?"

"Hanna," the third woman admonishes. Not unkindly. "You're not supposed to do that."

"Come *on*," Hanna says. "We were all *thinking it.*"

I can't help smiling. She's right; they probably all were.

"I wasn't," says another Wilder brother. This one is absurdly handsome, with a luminous smile. "Easton." He holds out his hand to shake. "You don't have to answer Hanna's question. She doesn't think she has to follow the rules of basic human politeness."

"But it would be rude not to answer me." Hanna aims a fierce laser gaze at Easton.

"The question was rude, so not answering it is a reasonable response," Easton says. "Ignore her," he tells me, all eye crinkles and white teeth and pretty boy smolder.

"No, it's okay," I say. "Yeah, I'm pregnant."

"How far along are you?"

The question comes from the third woman. Kane's sister, Amanda, the one in the photo on Kane's wall. Her eyes are almost exactly like Kane's—deep set and long-lashed.

"Thirty-two weeks—seven months and a bit." I hold my breath, waiting for someone to sound the alarm, but everyone is nodding and smiling in the general direction of my belly.

"I wish I'd looked half as good as you at seven months!" She sticks out her hand. "I'm Amanda."

"Amanda's the one who made this amazing meal," Clark says.

"It smells incredible," I say.

"Thank you!" Amanda says, beaming.

"The rest of us are on their way; we'll introduce you

when they get here. Dig in!" Clark says. "Before the food gets cold."

"You forgot Kane," Amanda points out.

I don't look at Kane. Or Clark.

I say, "Oh. We've met, out at the trailers, the first day I was here. And he was kind enough to offer to let me park my Airstream on his property." I'm pleased with how normal I sound.

"It's way closer to town than where the trailers are parked, and way quieter than parking it here," Kane puts in.

I definitely think the gentleman is protesting too much, but no one seems to notice. In fact, no one seems to have made any connection whatsoever between the state of my belly and the fact that Kane and I aren't strangers.

I think we've gotten away with all of it.

Until I catch the expression on Amanda's face. One perfectly plucked eyebrow is raised as high as it's possible for an eyebrow to go.

15

KANE

Mari lays a set of photographs on the table to start her presentation.

Everyone except me cranes to see the photos. I don't need to crane—or, like Hanna is doing, throw my body on the conference table—to see them. I've already seen them. Clark and I spent an hour yesterday talking about what bad news they were for us.

They're photos of glamping sites. Really fucking luxurious glamping sites. In Rush Creek.

Owned by a competitor.

"Ohhhhh," says Jessa, Clark's girlfriend, leaning in to look more closely. "Those are—amazing."

Clark glares at her.

"They *are* amazing," says Lucy, her hand capping Willow's sleeping head. "Gabe, we should book one of those for a getaway weekend!"

Another sharp Wilder brother glare.

Lucy and Jessa exchange glances, smiling.

"Where are the sites?" my brother Brody asks.

Clark rakes a hand through his hair. "On the Jensen brothers' land. Garth and Mick wanted to capitalize on the spa-and-wedding tourist crowd, too. So they pitched ten of these tents and are slowly reeling in customers."

"Well, shit," Brody and I say at the same time.

"Don't panic." And we all turn our attention to Mari. She's smiling. "I've got a plan. I know your original vision for the Airstreams was to make them luxury trailers. But if you do that, you'll be going toe to toe with these guys, and it'll be hard for you to stand out."

She's wearing an outfit that looks like layers and layers of scarves. It gives the impression of unfolding wings. Her rings, bracelets, and long earrings flash as she moves, but they're not as bright as her hair, which is, as always, down and in disarray. She's small, wild, and fierce, and just like that night in Vegas, I want to reach out and take her narrow wrists in my hands. Hold her still. Tame her and contain her, share in her completeness.

She looks around the table, meeting each of our eyes in turn. "Your Gilderness trips work because they combine two things that don't usually go together: luxury and survival. And people like that. It's different. People want to test themselves, but they don't want to suffer. No one else is doing it."

Another round of glances ping around the table; she's done her homework. Lucy and Gabe are impressed—not easy to accomplish.

"But straight up glamping? It's everywhere, now, and to win at it, you have to out-luxury everyone else. You don't want to go there, trust me. What you want to do what Gilderness, Brody's Boat, and your winter snowshoe-and-cocoa outings do so well—mix it up. Make it whimsical. Give people something they can't get anywhere else."

"Lavender sachets and A-frame shelters," Gabe murmurs to Lucy, and she gives him a thousand-watt smile.

Mari leans on the table—the pixie equivalent of the alpha male coming in for the kill. "I've done quite a few themed trailers in the past," she tells us. "And I think themed trailers would be perfect for what you're trying to accomplish."

"Themed trailers? Like, what, Elvis?" The scornful voice is, no surprise, Hanna's. She rolls her eyes.

But Brody's voice cuts across her objection. "Yes!" he says. "I can do theme nights on the boat and then we can upsell people on the trailers, or we could do combo packages."

We all turn to look at him.

You have to know Brody to know just how odd this is. Until Rachel came along, the Brody we knew didn't get excited about much—least of all marketing. He always had that bad boy go-ahead-and-try-to-raise-my-heart-rate thing going on. But right now, he looks like he's going to start jumping up and down.

And Rachel is nodding, too. "I love it."

"Me too," Lucy says.

Hanna scans the table, looking for an ally. Her eyes fall on me. And I don't know... I'm not all-in like Brody seemed instantly to be, but neither am I ready to side with Hanna and Clark—who's still scowling.

Before I can make up my mind, though, something entirely unexpected happens.

Gabe says, "That's *brilliant*."

16

MARI

They like it!

I mean, I knew they'd like it.

Of course I did.

But still. I savor the victory, just a little—especially Lucy's big smile of approval.

"Let's hear your ideas," Gabe says. "For themes."

"I'd rather hear yours to start." I mean it. I want as many ideas as possible to come from the Wilders. "Throw out some ideas you think your audience would appreciate."

"The Mandalorian. Grogu," Amanda says quickly. "Though maybe I'm overly influenced by what my kids are obsessed with."

"No, good one."

"Could we actually do an Elvis trailer? Oh, or, what about the Beatles?"

That's Kane's mom, Barb, who's sitting next to her girlfriend Geneva—two silver-haired middle-aged women holding hands under the table.

"We could do just about anything."

"I'm worried about the demographic," Lucy says, brow furrowed.

"She's saying you're an old fart," Geneva tells Barb fondly.

"I am *not!*" Lucy says.

Barb smiles at her daughter-in-law across the table. "I mean, it's not like I *listened* to Elvis or the Beatles when they were popular. But aren't they kind of evergreen?"

"Evergreen is great," I say, "because you don't want to have to reno every few years when things fall out of fashion. But you also want to do an interior redesign at least every ten years, and you may need to do it sooner depending on volume. So I'd suggest a mix of evergreen and trendy."

"The Avengers," Brody says. He may be tattooed like a bad boy and wearing leather and motorcycle boots, but he was the first brother to chime in and say he loved my idea, so I'm warm and fuzzy for anything he suggests.

"I'm trying to picture Avengers night on the boat," Rachel says. She's Brody's fiancée, the one who sells sex toys and is in the process of becoming a sex therapist. Obviously, I need to get to know her better.

"Sex toy recs from Thor and Loki," Brody says.

"Omigod I would totally go to that," I say.

Kane makes a choking sound. Clark claps him on the back. "Swallowed my water wrong," Kane says.

"Fifties diner," Rachel suggests, and then suddenly, the Wilders are suggesting one idea after another out like time's running out: *The Last Airbender. Schitt's Creek. TikTok.*

The Mars Rover. Bitcoin.

"Bitcoin?" Gabe demands. "Over my cold, dead body. That shit is environmental disaster."

I'm writing as fast as I can. I shed my bracelets so I can write faster.

"Barbie!" Rachel calls. "Dream Camper."

"Ohhhhh," Jessa says. "I want to stay in that one."

"So do I." Lucy is all smiles.

"Ding ding ding, we have a winner," Clark announces.

I guess I've won him over. A Barbie theme was on my list, too. I have a board for it and lots of sketches. So for sure, *I* have a winner.

"Bridgerton," Hanna says.

We all turn to look at her.

She clamps her mouth shut and turns a ferocious shade of red. I assume it's because she was my strongest holdout just a few minutes earlier. Then I get a load of the look on Lucy's face.

"Hanna," Lucy intones. "Did you watch a television show based on a romance novel?"

Easton begins laughing. Hard.

"Shut. Up." Hanna tells him.

"I can't! You watched *Bridgerton*!"

"*Bridgerton* is hot," Rachel says. "I would totally sleep in a *Bridgerton* trailer."

"You wouldn't do much sleeping," Brody murmurs to her, forcing us all to pretend we didn't hear him. Rachel blushes.

Lucy leans forward. "You could totally do that inn room where they first—"

"Shhh, no spoilers," Geneva says. "Barb and I are only on the third episode of the first season."

"So much goodness ahead for you." Rachel is looking dreamy-eyed and fanning herself.

Hanna mumbles something.

"What?" Rachel asks.

"The duke's ass," she enunciates.

Easton has stopped laughing and is watching Hanna. As if he's never seen her before.

No one else seems to notice. They've all returned to riffing.

"*Downton Abbey*," Lucy suggests. "*Twilight. Outlander.* Christian Grey's red room."

Kane's brow furrows. "What's that?"

The women exchange glances.

"You know," Lucy says. "*Fifty Shades of Grey.*"

"Mmm." I shiver. "I'd book that one."

Kane makes a small, rough sound.

I look at him and remember the moment he backed me against the wall in the bathroom, my wrists held in one of his hands, over my head.

His eyes pin me in place. He's remembering, too—this time I'm absolutely sure.

Mmm. Mmm-hmm.

Aaand. Back to business.

"Okay," I say. "Let me show you some boards and drawings to get a sense of whether we're all picturing this the same way..."

"THAT WAS A GREAT SALES PITCH," Lucy says when the meeting is done. Her daughter is still conked out in the wrap on her chest.

The Wilder brothers have scattered, while the women have stayed at the table and pulled their chairs up to surround me. It's a little overwhelming for someone who doesn't spend a lot of time with people, but it's also flattering. They're giving off a clear *welcome* vibe—and that's something I don't experience very often.

"Thanks," I tell her. "I love what you've done with the business. Obviously I can't exactly see where it was before you started, but I can intuit, and it's impressive."

"There are a lot of talented businesswomen in this room," Lucy says. "We probably should start a secondary business helping other women grow their small businesses."

"YouTube channel!" Jessa says.

Rachel claps. "That would be really cool! We could bring business in for all of us, and for Wilder, too."

"Let's do it!" Jessa turns to direct a question to me. "Would you be interested?"

"I mean, I'm only here temporarily."

"That's what they *all* say," Hanna says darkly.

"What who all says?"

"All the girlfriends when they come to town. Lucy said it. Rachel said it. Jessa said it. And now you."

Lucy leaps in. "She's not saying you're anyone's girlfriend. I mean, obviously you're someone's girlfriend, or wife, or... sperm donation recipient..." She blushes and inclines her head toward my belly, then gives me an extremely sheepish look. "Ugh. I should just shut up before I make it any worse." Her cheeks are bright pink.

"Don't worry about it," I tell her. "I get what you were trying to say. And, no, it wasn't an immaculate conception. But I'm not 'with-with' the dad." I crook my fingers around "with-with" and deliberately don't look at Kane.

I *don't* look at him so fiercely that it feels like a presence in the room.

Lucy gives me a grateful smile. I really like her. Her, Rachel, Amanda, Jessa—even Hanna with her refreshing bluntness.

"You know what I meant, though," Hanna says to Lucy, accusingly. "All of you were planning to leave. You all thought you were just here temporarily, and then, next thing you know, you're all in love with a Wilder and ready to settle down and make Rush Creek your home."

Four heads swing around my way.

"Not me!" My laugh comes out just a little too forceful.

My pronouncement is greeted with four dubious looks.

"Kane seemed very interested in your comment about sex toys," Rachel says, all innocent eyes.

"That's only because men don't think women have sex lives when they're not in the room," I say quickly.

"Well, that's definitely true," Jessa says, laughing.

The baby kicks, and I settle my hand over my belly. And despite my best intentions, my gaze searches the room for Kane.

He's taking photos again—of his brothers clustered together, chatting—but he must feel my eyes on him, because he looks up and smiles. And holy shit, that smile.

Worse, still, when the smile fades, he's still looking at me, and there's so much heat in his gaze that my body blazes.

He lifts his phone, a question. I nod an okay, and he holds the phone up, capturing a photo. Or several. Is he photographing me? Or the whole group of us? Should it matter?

When I look back at the women, they're all staring at me. Curiously.

Uh-oh.

"Why don't you join us for our next family dinner?" Jessa asks.

"I, uh..."

"It's next weekend—Saturday, a week from tomorrow."

Amanda beams. "Yes! Jessa, isn't your family going to be here that weekend? It'll be a party!"

"As opposed to the other Wilder dinners, which are small family affairs," Jessa says dryly to Rachel. To me she says, "When the Wilders have 'family dinner,' it's like most people's Thanksgivings. But at least once a month. And with a lot more Korean and Cuban food. My mom's family's Korean, and Rachel's Cuban American. And the Wilders are like all of Anglo-Saxony had a love child, except they were probably Italian in another life if the spaghetti sauce is anything to go by."

I laugh. "Don't monthly Thanksgivings take a lot of energy?"

"Everyone pitches in," Lucy says. "Many hands make light work."

Jessa crosses her arms. "My parents would love to meet you. They've always talked about buying an Airstream. You should come."

"Yes," says Rachel. "You're coming."

I hesitate, but this is what Kane wanted: for me to get a sense for the family that this baby would grow up in, if it were raised here. I'm sure he'd want me to say yes to the invitation. And let's be honest, it's not exactly an invitation anymore, with the four of them staring at me. It's a mandate.

Still, I'm pretty sure the reason I want to say yes to dinner—and I *do*—isn't because of those stares. Or because I want to evaluate Kane's family.

It's because I like these women.

And part of me craves what they're offering—easy acceptance.

Friendship.

And that—the craving—scares me more than a little.

17

KANE

I need help, I text Amanda.

What kind of help?

I hesitate, weighing different considerations. How much I want my sister's help—against how much I don't want to raise her suspicions.

The need for help wins out.

I want to celebrate Mari's victory.

What she did today was the Wilder family equivalent of one of those obstacle course races where survival, not victory, is the point. It's tough enough to run the meet-the-Wilder gauntlet—but she also made a business proposal and got Gabe—fucking Gabe!—to use the word "brilliant."

I mean, that has to be some kind of Wilder family first. Even Lucy never got a *brilliant*.

Probably not even when she gave birth to his daughter.

I make an internal note: *Tell Mari she's brilliant after she pushes the baby out.*

But meanwhile, I want to do something to celebrate her victory, and I know what it has to be.

Boston fucking cream pie.

I think it must be some kind of primitive male mammal thing. Like, if I can bring my woman the woolly mammoth she needs, or in this case, the Boston cream pie she craves, she will know that I am a good provider and allow me to care for her and her offspring.

Absurd, obviously.

But here I am, texting my sister, the person most likely to see through my barely veiled secret, to ask for help with my mission.

I need to make a Boston cream pie.

Why?

I start to type, *None of your business*, then realize that if I want my sister's help, I probably shouldn't piss her off. Which is reinforced when her next text says, *If you want my help, you need to tell me.*

It's for Mari. She told me she's having a pregnancy craving for it.

Long silence, during which I imagine that she is texting all of our other siblings as well as her closest friends and every gossip in Rush Creek: *Kane wants to make a Boston cream pie for Mari!*

My phone buzzes *I know,* Amanda texts back. *Nan told me.*

Then why did you ask???????

To piss you off. Is it working?

Oh my God. Siblings.

Yes, it's working. Now, can you help me?

Of course I can help you. But you have to admit you like her.

Okay. I like her, I say, because it's true. Because it's easier than arguing. And because my need to give Mari this Boston cream pie is savage.

I'm in the Around the Table kitchen, she texts. *Get your ass over here.*

"WHAT THE HELL?" Amanda says, looking at the flat disk we've just pulled from the oven. She picks up the recipe. "You must have forgotten the baking powder."

"Oh, *shit*," I say.

"How can you forget the baking powder?"

My arm is tired from whisking custard and beating the frosting—which is apparently called ganache. I haven't baked anything this complicated since I was about twelve years old, and I know exactly how I forgot the baking powder. Fantasizing about the way Mari would moan around her fork when she put the first bite of my Boston cream pie in her mouth.

Amanda must intuit this—or something like it—because she sighs and says, "My brothers are such idiots when it comes to women. All right. Start over, dude. I'm sorry. But it'll give the custard more time to cool."

I scrape the ruined cake into the trash and queue up the ingredients for a second attempt.

"She couldn't have wanted pickles and ice cream like everyone else," I mutter, as I beat the cake batter for the second time.

"She definitely seems like she paddles her own canoe," Amanda says.

I squint at her.

"I just mean, living on the road, designing RVs for a living. The way she dresses. She's her own person. I like that about her."

I give up trying to figure out if Amanda's trolling me. "I like that about her, too," I say. Then, "What?" because of the way Amanda is looking at me.

"Kane," she says.

"What?" I repeat.

"To reiterate. *Living on the road. Designing RVs for a living.* She's not a settle-down-and-fall-in-love girl."

I cross my arms. "I *know* that."

Amanda's expression softens. "I know you know that," she says. "My big question is, does your *heart* know that?" She gestures with her fancy caterer's spoon in the direction of my second attempt. "This is a lot of work to get laid. Even for a Wilder." She scrunches up one corner of her mouth. "And you're not a one-and-done guy. You fall. You fall hard."

I can't say anything back to her, because she's just laid out my problem in a nutshell.

"I'll be okay," I insist.

She gives me another long look, then shakes her head.

"Pay attention to that cake," she says. "You don't want to have to bake a third one."

18

MARI

There's a knock on Bernadette's door.

It pulls me out of deep concentration on the trailer project and sends a small thrill of anticipation up my spine.

Kane.

It's gotta be Kane. It's not like I get visitors.

I haul myself off the couch—an increasingly challenging undertaking. Even though I know it has to be him, I peep out. One of the awesome mods on Bernadette, courtesy of her previous owner, is a peephole, which is super useful when you're a single woman on the road alone.

And even though I know it has to be him, I still feel a surge of pleased surprise when I see his face.

"Delivery," he says, holding out a big, round Tupperware... cake holder? "Boston cream pie."

Holy shit, he found it.

I yank open the door and have to stop myself from snatching the cake out of his hands. Or throwing my arms around him and hugging the crap out of him. "Where did you find it?"

"I—"

He stops, appearing to think better of whatever he was about to say, but it's too late. I know where that sentence was going.

"You *made* it?"

"Amanda helped," he says, like that's going to take anything away from a six-foot-something built-like-a-God man who *bakes Boston cream pies.*

"Aaaaahhhh!" I cry, overcome. "You are a saint and a genius."

He tries to bite back a smile. "I think you're overstating things a little."

"No," I say, shaking my head. I have been fantasizing about yellow custard, soft yellow cake, and chocolate ganache nonstop since before I knew Kane had planted this baby in me. "Come in. You have to have some, too."

"It's all for you," he says. "I wouldn't take any of your special treat. Your presentation was fantastic. You deserve all the cake."

This guy. I swear. He was too much in Vegas, when all I knew about him was that he asked real questions and knew how to use his body for both good and evil. Now...

"Well, come in anyway."

He hesitates again, then follows me in, setting the cake on the counter. I remove my bracelets, wash my hands, and take two small plates down from the cabinets. I grab two forks from the utensil drawer, and two mugs from the over-head hooks. "I don't have coffee—" I gesture at my belly, "—but I have tea, milk, or water."

"Water would be great," he says. "And no cake. I'm serious. It's yours."

I wrestle the cake carrier open and cut into my prize. My mouth waters as I do. It's so—

Not gonna say *moist*, but holy shit, it soooo is.

"Can I look at these?" he asks.

I look up to see him touching my bracelets where I left them on the kitchen counter.

"Sure."

"This one. You always fidget with it." He picks it up and reads aloud the inscription. "*Not all those who wander are lost.*" He smiles. "Tolkien, huh?"

"My mom gave it to me. When I was twelve. Not too long before she left."

He sets the bracelet down. "But you still wear it."

"I didn't for a while. And then I wanted to again. Because I believe it's true."

His eyes move slowly over my face; I've seen that expression on his face before, when he's taking photographs. He's *seeing*. It makes me feel both warm and a little nervous. What, exactly, is he seeing?

"It doesn't get lonely? Living like that?"

I shake my head. That's an easy question. "Not for me. It makes me happy."

He seems to chew on that, his gaze moving from my face to someplace far away, past it.

We sit at Bernadette's little pink dinette table. I'd forgotten how small this table is with two people at it. Or maybe it's how big Kane is; his knees touch mine, and his arms cover so much territory, even with his hands folded. I force myself to look away because staring at close range is both rude and dangerous.

His eyes are very, very blue.

I dig in. "Oh, wow," I say. "Wow."

It's soft. Moist (again, sorry!). Tender, springy. The custard is cool and smooth on my tongue, the ganache dark and flavorful.

"Mmm. Just. Thank you."

Kane grins at me, like he's pleased, though there's something else in his expression I can't quite read. "I did good?"

"You did amazing. So good I could kiss you."

One eyebrow goes up, but he only says, "How does it rate among the Boston cream pies of the world?"

"It's up there. Although pregnancy *might* be biasing me." I lick a bite that's mostly custard from my fork, and catch a glimpse of Kane's face. His eyes are... interested. I lick again, for good measure, and notice the muscle in his jaw tense.

A ripple of tension slides down the lower slope of my belly and lodges itself in my internal muscles. In their constantly primed state, they... quiver dangerously.

The next time I look at him, Kane's eyes are on my chest. I'm wearing a flowy green maternity dress with a low scoop neck, and, why, yes, it does show off my newly ridiculously huge boobs to excellent advan—

"You have—"

He reaches out. "Some cake—"

His finger almost touches the upper curve of my breast, and, oh, whoops, yes, that is cake on my boob. I use my own finger to scoop it up, then lick it clean.

I hear the moment the breath leaves Kane's lungs.

I see the moment his gaze travels from my chest to my mouth, when it fixes on my finger, sliding between my lips. The moment it sticks, and stays, right there on my mouth, even as my hand drops away.

"Mari—"

His voice is hoarse.

"Do it. Just—do it," I order him.

Then he's leaning over the table, setting his mouth over mine, hot and unhesitating and so, so good.

I go up in flames. I drop the fork with a clatter, grab his arms across the table, moaning and whimpering my approval. And he responds like he's been electrified, devouring my sounds, plundering my mouth, his tongue sliding against mine.

And then, as quickly as he started it, he breaks the kiss.

He collapses back in his seat with a groan. Licks his bottom lip. And, fuck me, I can't take my eyes off his blown pupils and puffy just-kissed mouth...

By the time I organize my brain enough to get my bearings, Kane has pushed himself up and slid out of his seat.

I follow his gaze. His eyes rest on my bracelet, still sitting on the kitchen counter, then track back to my face.

"I'm sorry," he says.

"You're—sorry?" I demand. Because, you know. No one should *ever* say that after a kiss.

"Not—that I—I'm not sorry I kissed you. God, no." His eyes get bigger, darker. "Let me just repeat that. I wouldn't unkiss you for the world."

That makes me snort-laugh, even as my body is seizing up in preparation for disappointment. *No, Miss Horny Pants, not for you, not today.*

"But it's a terrible idea. I shouldn't have."

"I mean, the damage is kind of *done*," I tease, waving a hand over my belly.

That makes him smile.

"It wasn't as good as you remembered?" I'm half teasing, half not.

At that, his pupils get even bigger.

"Ah. No. I mean, yes. I mean—Jesus, Mari, I can't answer that. That *night*…"

His words, but even more, the tone of his voice, send a surge of heat and tingles straight to my already-swollen sex.

"Me too," I whisper.

His eyes are fierce on me, and for a second, I think he's coming back for more, and my entire body thrills at the possibility. But at the last minute, he sighs, and his gaze falls to the table. Then meets mine, frank and warm. "What I like, what I want, really doesn't matter right now. There are more important things at stake than…"

He doesn't finish the sentence, and impishly, I do: "Than how hot that kiss was?"

He groans. "Mari."

"I mean, it was extremely hot."

The color is high in his cheeks, and his pupils have blotted out most of the blue in his eyes. "You are *not* helping."

"It depends what you're trying to achieve," I point out. I know I'm not being fair.

He's quiet for a moment, like he's thinking really hard about that. And that, right there?

That's one of the things I like so, so much about Kane.

"We're both trying to figure out how this baby should

grow up. And that includes the question of…" He hesitates and turns away from me. "Whether its parents are a couple or not. Not whether or not we're attracted to each other, because I think we can both agree"—his eyes meet mine again, dark and hungry, setting up an answering longing in me—"that we are. But whether you want to be here. Permanently here. That's very much up in the air."

I nod, because as much as I don't want to admit it right now with the taste of his mouth and the feel of his hands still vivid, he's absolutely right.

"And I don't want to cloud either of our judgements. I'm trying to do the right thing," he says finally.

Of course he is. I'm starting to get the impression that Kane Wilder will do the right thing no matter what.

And even though that's frustrating right this second, it's also exactly what I need from him.

More importantly? It's what this baby needs from him.

I take a deep breath, stow my horniness for the thousandth time since I've arrived in Rush Creek, and smile at him.

"I know. And as much as I hate to admit it, I also know you're right."

That doesn't mean I don't want another of those kisses. Or a hundred more.

19

KANE

"Oh, hey, Mari!" Clark says.

My head shoots up from where my chin was practically resting on my chest. I'm sitting at the Wilder conference table with my brothers and Hanna, trying to stay awake as we plow through a bunch of minor business issues. Mari has just stepped through the doors of Wilder headquarters and is ambling towards us. Even in the last two weeks that she's been here, her walk has changed. I wouldn't quite call it a waddle, but it's adorable.

My caveman-self desperately wants to put one hand on the small of her back and escort her everywhere.

As to why I was almost asleep at the conference table?

I haven't gotten nearly as much sleep the last few nights as I would have liked.

It's been four days since I kissed Mari in her RV. Since then, I've tried to mostly stay out of her way, except for dropping off breakfast every morning, but I haven't been able to stop thinking about what happened. There's plenty of material there. The curve of her generous breasts in the scoop of her dress, the sight of her finger stroking across that creamy flesh and then delving between her soft lips—

Then, her voice, a plea:

Do it. Just—do it.

I will hear those words every night in my dreams. In fact, I *have* heard them every night in my fantasies, a little catch of desperation in her voice but utter certainty, too. No hesitation at all.

Then the kiss—a whimper, a moan, her hands clutching my arms, her mouth already open, her tongue clashing with mine.

But the instant my brain clicked back in, I remembered the bracelet. What it said about who she was. A wanderer.

And I remembered why we were both there. For the baby.

Mari sits down in a chair that Clark holds out for her.

"You have an update for us?" he asks, right off.

"Everything's on track," she says. "I've got contractor meetings all this week, and then I'll head to Salt Lake City on Monday to grab that range we talked about—"

Screeeeeech!

"Wait, back up," I say.

Her eyes flick to mine, but when she speaks, she addresses Clark. "There's a guy in Salt Lake with an almost new bright red range I want for Christian Grey's red room." She says it as if it's a sentence that makes sense. "I have to go pick it up."

No! She can't leave town. I haven't yet convinced her that the baby—*our* baby—should be raised here—and by both of us.

If I hadn't known that I had my work cut out for me *before* I saw the inscription inside her bracelet, I know it now.

I need all the time I can get.

"Let's send someone with her," Gabe says.

"I'll go." It pops right out of my mouth.

Gabe shakes his head. "I still need to see snow trip proposals from you and Hanna."

"I can get those done before we go. I can have mine to you tomorrow."

Even *I* can hear the desperation in my voice. I know she can. She's watching me now, an amused expression on her face.

Gabe appears to consider it, then shakes his head again. "Clark says you've been indispensable out at the trailer office."

Damn me for being useful. I should have known better.

"I can go," another voice offers.

No. *No, ani, nyet, non, nee, nein,* nope, nope, nope. *No fucking way.*

The *I can go*, of course, is Easton's. Also, it turns out that I said the *no fucking way* part out loud. But my words have —blessedly—been drowned out by another set of words— Hanna's.

"Of *course* Easton wants to go. Pretty girl, small RV, only one bed, getting out of work for a week, what's not to love?"

Hanna has successfully diverted attention away from me and my outburst. The only person in the room still looking at me with raised eyebrows is Clark. I shake my head at him, and he shakes his back. He's smirking at me. I scowl. He smirks harder.

Fucking brothers.

"I'm trying to be helpful, Han," Easton says reasonably.

"You're trying to win over the new girl to the cause of worshipping at the altar of Easton," Hanna says.

I have never loved her as much as I do right now.

"The new girl is sitting right here," Mari says, but her mouth is curled with amusement.

"I would *never*," Easton tells Hanna.

She rolls her eyes at him.

"Easton has to plan for summer season, doesn't he?" I ask. "I don't think he's shown us all his summer plan yet. Have you, Easton?"

Easton gives me wounded look. I've just thrown him under the bus. There's a code of honor among us younger brothers on that point. No feeding brothers to the wolves, or the wolf. Gabe.

Unless there's a woman involved. Then all bets are off.

"That's true, Eas," Gabe says sternly. There should be a new adverb for the tone of voice and body language that goes with Gabe's stern attention. *Gabely.* He looks around the table. "Okay. Kane. If you can really get the snow trip proposal done early next week, I'll send you. Assuming that's okay with you, Mari."

I can't read the expression on her face, but in the hopes of staving off any protest, I add, "I'll be tenting on the road, so no need to worry about sleeping quarters."

The corner of her mouth quivers. I think she's trying not to laugh.

"Works for me," she tells Gabe.

I throw a triumphant look in Easton's direction. He narrows his eyes at me. *I'm getting you back for that.*

It's fine; I'm not scared of Easton. He's never done anything *Gabely* in his life.

As we're all getting up from the table, I catch Clark's eye again. He gives me an air fist bump.

I return his nod.

But even as I celebrate the victory, I wonder if it's really a victory. After all, what have I won?

"Thank you."

I spin around to find Mari standing right behind me, so close I can feel the warmth radiating off her skin. "I'm sure Easton would also have made an excellent companion, but it makes more sense for you to come with me, since we already know each other."

Pretty sure she's smirking at me. Pretty sure she put extra emphasis on *know*.

"And it's flattering you were willing to go to the mat to be the one to accompany me," she says. "*No fucking way*," she whispers, imitating me.

"You heard that."

"I might have."

"I just—" But I've got nothing.

"Jealousy's cute on you," she says.

I'm still sputtering, trying to come up with a comeback, as she walks away and out of the office.

Yeah. I've won the right to spend several days on the road in a very small space with a woman I can't keep my hands off of...

And know I'm not supposed to touch.

20

MARI

Tonight is the Wilder family dinner.

Lucy and company weren't kidding about the size of this soirée. The Wilder lot is full of cars. I park Bernadette—Kane came earlier, and I needed a nap. Approaching the front porch, I see the party spilling out onto it and hear the din of lots of people talking and laughing. A bevy of kids races around the front of the house from the back, followed by a big fluffy mutt, then disappears around the other side.

As I take another step, I feel an unnerving sensation, and it has nothing to do with the kids or any Wilder. It's the result of my being a strong candidate for a wardrobe malfunction.

Earlier this evening, I realized I had no pants that fit. Which happened overnight. I put on my last pair of leggings, but while I was finishing up getting ready, the waistband rolled down and snuck under my belly, like my pants were retreating in fear. Still, optimistically, I decided they would be okay. It was just one evening.

But with each step I take toward the porch, they slide lower on my ass.

And I can't flee. I've been spotted. Lucy separates herself from a group of guests or family or both and comes to greet me with a big smile. She's been great to me this week—she introduced me to the OB/GYN practice she's used—even gave them a heads-up call to convince them to see me on short notice, so I could make a Rush Creek-based birth plan. She also found me a friend's Airbnb at a good price, to get me through the period right before and right after the birth—since I will need comfier digs then.

"Hey!" she says. "You made it. Okay, so, don't be intimidated. I'm going to make sure you know who everyone is. And you won't be quizzed."

"I, um, might need a minute—" I lean in and explain the situation to her, that I need to go back to my Airstream and change.

She giggles. "I have soooo been there. And I'd lend you some of my stuff, except I think you could put two of you in my maternity clothes. Go change," she says, and shoos me off.

When I return, I'm wearing the only thing that seems to fit—the green dress from the day Kane brought me the Boston cream pie. The one I was wearing when he kissed me. Which feels...

Well, fraught.

But beggars can't be choosers. Especially when they're pregnant.

Lucy's waiting. She links arms with me and leads me into the fray. "Just remember, no one expects you to remember all our names or who we go with."

"Thank you," I whisper, and she gives me a friendly sideways smile.

Lots of introductions follow. Lucy's great about reminding me who people are, but I quickly lose track. All I remember is that three of the kids belong to Amanda and her husband Heath (who I also meet), and one to Brody and Rachel. Gabe has the baby, Willow, strapped to his chest, which is... really, really stinkin' adorable.

"Here," Rachel says, appearing from nowhere and shoving a glass of something into my hand. "I assumed no alcohol, so this is non-alcoholic sparkling cider."

I smile, gratefully, and drink, trying to catch my breath.

We end up in the kitchen, where there's some kind of complex pizza operation going on.

"Want to help?" Kane asks. He's spreading sauce on a circle of dough. "It's a make-your-own pizza assembly line. We need someone to sprinkle cheese."

"Yes!" Small talk makes me squirmy and it's way easier for me to be myself if I have my hands full.

He pushes a saucy dough circle my way and hands me a huge, industrial-kitchen-sized bowl of mozzarella cheese.

Watching the Wilders in action, I pass a few happy minutes as cheese master. Amanda has wandered in with a small boy at her side and set him up at the table. She leans over and cuts his pizza into bite sized pieces, then hands him a small fork. A few minutes later, Gabe strolls in, frees Willow from her carrier, and drops her into a high chair. He sits across from her with a small bowl and spoon and, as she hoots with delight, shovels baby food into her wide-open baby bird mouth.

Still in the pizza assembly line, I sprinkle cheese and

push my finished product to Jessa, who adds toppings. I'm grateful to have something to do because I'm feeling a little overwhelmed.

"Oh, *shit,*" Gabe says suddenly. "Literally, shit. I think I've got a diaper blowout on my hands here. Can someone get Luce? This is a two-man job. Three, maybe, if you count her face."

Willow's beaming face is *covered* with baby food. It's in her eyebrows and hair.

"Let Luce relax," Amanda says. "I'll get it." She starts to get up, but Kane puts a hand on her shoulder and pushes her down.

"You're on your feet 24/7," he says. "Let me get it."

"Willow," Gabe tells his happily babbling daughter. "There are people lining up to change your diaper. You're a super star."

Kane dampens a washcloth and strides to Gabe and Willow's aid. He bends down and begins removing rice cereal and sweet potatoes from Willow's face and hands, as she erupts into protests.

"Who's my pretty girl?" he coos to her, booping her nose with the washcloth. "Peek-a-boo!" he says, and suddenly she's smiling again, letting him finish with her face.

I look around to see if the other women seem to think any of this behavior is odd. Like, maybe he's putting on a show for me. If I were him, I'd be putting on a show for me.

Jessa intercepts my searching look and smiles. "He's always like this," she says, as if I'd asked my question aloud. "Kane *adores* Willow."

Between them, Gabe and Kane wrestle Willow out of

her seat and carry her off into the next room for a diaper change. I crane my neck.

Jessa smiles at me and shoves a plate with a hot piece of pizza into my hands. "Take a break and eat," she says. "I'll do cheese until you're ready to take over again. We're slowing down, so I can manage *both* toppings *and* cheese."

I wander in the direction Kane went. He and Gabe have a whole operation going on there. Willow lies on a changing mat on a towel on the floor. The two men have a system of wipes and washcloths. Kane is collecting some of the foulest clothes I have ever seen into a plastic bag. "Can I burn these?" he asks Gabe, who laughs.

"I wish," Gabe says. "Throw them straight into the washer, and make sure you close and latch it, or Buck will—"

"Please don't finish that thought," Kane says, but he's laughing, too, elbowing his brother and teasing Willow.

Any other woman, I think. Any other woman would see this and hold out her ring finger. Any other woman would park her RV in his driveway and stay for the rest of her life.

I realize, suddenly, that my chest is tight, that it's hard to draw a full breath. I think I must make a sound, because Kane turns around and sees me. He smiles, and then—realizing I'm struggling, he starts to rise to his feet.

"I'm okay," I say. "I just need some air."

I set my plate of pizza on a nearby shelf and hurry outside.

21

KANE

I follow Mari outside to the side of the house.

She leans against the wall and draws a deep breath. Then another. She's twisting the bracelet on her wrist. I know her well enough now to be pretty sure it's a tell. She feels trapped.

"You okay?" I ask.

She nods.

"What happened?"

"You're all so... good at it—at everything," she says. "Good with kids, good with family, good with each other. What if... What if I can't do that?"

My heart does a funny flip thing in my chest. Because if I'm not wrong, it sounds a little bit like she's trying to imagine herself into our lives.

And yes, she's terrified that she won't measure up... but that doesn't change the fact that she's letting herself think about it.

"You don't have to be any special way," I say.

Her eyes meet mine, and they're a little damp. "I just

don't know if I have it in me, you know? My mom never changed her mind. I thought she might when we went to live near my aunt, but then—"

Her mouth opens, but no more words come. Her eyes shine in the light coming from the porch.

"Then she left," I fill in.

She draws another breath, twists the bracelet. "Yeah. She came back for birthdays and Christmas for a while, but she was always antsy. It was like she was counting down the minutes until she could get on the road again. It made me antsy, too. I would beg her to take me with her this time..."

My heart breaks for teenaged Mari, begging her mother to be taken along. No wonder Mari doesn't want a repeat of that with her own child.

"After a while, she just made excuses and didn't come back." She looks down at the ground. My eyes follow hers and I notice that she's barefoot. She must have kicked off her shoes inside the house at some point.

She sighs. "The thing is, it sucks that she left me, but I get it now. There are some people who aren't meant to be tied down."

Even though she sounds resigned, I'm pretty sure somewhere inside, that little girl is still there, hoping.

She touches her fingertips to her lower lip. "Some people fantasize about getting married, having babies, big families, everyone jostling and helping—like in there." She gestures back at the house. "That would be so many women's fantasy. I fantasize about the inside of my Airstream. Quiet. Clean. Just the way I want it."

Her eyes come up to meet mine. They're open and honest. She's not hiding from me, and as much as it hurts that she doesn't want what I want, I'm grateful for what she's giving me. I'm sure she doesn't open up like this often.

"That's okay," I tell her. "It's okay."

There are tears on her cheeks, I realize. I reach out and gently brush them away.

A strange expression crosses her face. At first, I think it's because I'm touching her, but it's something else. She shocks me by reaching for my hand. Before I can register what she's doing, she lays my palm flat on her belly. Her all-who-wander bracelet clicks against a beaded one. "The baby's kicking."

My heart thuds, hard. Her belly is firmer than I expected, taut, almost, and under my hand, something ripples, strong and fierce. Then again, rolling against my palm. I gasp, my eyes going to hers. "Mari—"

I'm sure she'll look away, but she looks right back, holding my gaze. I can't move and I can't look away—and I don't want to. I feel like she's spun magic around me. The electric triple sensation, of her warm skin under her dress, the baby's movement, and her hand over mine—I feel it all the way up my arm, in my chest, an avalanche of sensation and emotion.

My baby.

"Yes," Mari says, because I've apparently said it out loud.

Then I hear: "Kane?"

It's Amanda's voice. I jerk my hand off Mari's belly, but it's too late. My sister stares at me, wide-eyed, fascinated. Her eyes slide to Mari and back to me again, putting the pieces together.

"It's... *yours?*"

I open my mouth to say something, anything, some form of protest or denial, but of course that's absolutely absurd. It *is* mine.

And it's too late, anyway. She's been followed around the corner by my mom, and just a few yards behind her, Hanna and Easton.

I look at Mari. Her hand is still on her own belly, and I watch her fingers ripple with the movement beneath. She stares back at me. She looks calm, now, like whatever storm brought her out of the house has passed. She gives me a slight nod. I ask her one more time, searching out her eyes: *Are you sure?* and she nods again.

I try to tell her, back, *It'll be okay. I know they're a lot, but you're safe with them.*

Then I turn back to where my family waits, all curiosity and patience.

"Yeah," I say. "It's mine."

22

___

KANE

They surround us, everyone talking at once. My mother, exclaiming, fretting. Amanda wide-eyed and almost gleeful, going on about *more cousins, more cousins*. Hanna, of course, full of questions.

"Wait," Hanna says. "That's *your* baby in there? How—?"

"Well, Hanna," Easton says. "When a man and a woman love each other very much, they do a special kind of lying-down and the man—"

"Oh, because you have so much experience with love and the special kind of lying-down, Mr. Quantity-Over-Quality?" Hanna demands.

Before Easton can respond—and I know there's a response coming, because I can see the mischief behind his eyes—I interrupt.

"It was last summer. In Vegas."

"Ohhhhh," says Amanda. "That's why you were so weird and mopey after that trip."

"He was weird and mopey?" Hanna asks. "I didn't notice."

"He was." Amanda crosses her arms. "Totally."

"I just—"

But there's not much I can say. I want to deny it, but Amanda's right. That single, brief encounter with Mari rocked my world, and for weeks afterwards, things felt colorless and bland, like my real life was just out of reach. I wanted a repeat, which was impossible. And even if it hadn't been impossible, it was a terrible idea, because why would she want a repeat? What chance was there that a repeat would live up to the first time? And even if it did, why would I possibly think there was enough between us to sustain a relationship?

A relationship.

That's right, folks. One night, just a little under an hour from start to finish, including the conversation, and I wanted *more*. Not just more sex, but more-more.

I'd gone in channeling Easton and come out—

Welp, *boy next door* all the way.

I just can't slough off that part of myself.

And right now, I don't want to. I want to embrace the hell out of it.

"Oh, man," Amanda says. "I so should have known when you wanted to bake Boston cream pie. You never baked Boston cream pie for Veronica or Betsy or Lacey—"

"That's enough of *that*," I say, alarmed by the growing list of my uninspired choices, which Mari really doesn't need to hear.

"Ha! Now you know how it feels to be me!" Easton crows.

"No," Hanna says. "Because he's a serial monogamist, and you're a serial—what is even the word for that? Fuck-tologist?" She scowls at Easton. "Did you just look *proud* at that?"

"It sounds... skilled," he says with a shrug. "Fucktologist," he muses. "Better than panty melter."

"You are such a..." She sputters to a halt before she can finish the sentence.

"I'm just so glad it's you!" Amanda tells Mari, who looks increasingly wide-eyed and terrified. "I've liked you since the minute I met you. You'll make such a completely awesome addition to our girls' nights, and your baby won't be much younger than Willow—we're going to have such a—"

"Amanda!"

Four pairs of wide, shocked eyes find my face. They have never, not once, heard me snap.

On the other hand, I have also never gotten someone pregnant.

It's a big year for personal growth, for better or for worse.

I cross my arms and rack my brains for a way to spin this that gives Mari some room to breathe.

"You're not—together."

It's not a question.

It's my mother's voice, and her disappointed, I-just-want-the-best-for-my-kids Mom face.

I can't stop myself, and look at Mari again, and oh, my God, she looks like she's going to throw up. Or run. This wasn't how this was supposed to go down. Not at all. I'm supposed to be giving her space, letting her figure this out.

I'm supposed to convince her to fall in love with my family, not let them scare the shit out of her.

"No," I say. "We're not together. I didn't even know she was pregnant until two weeks ago. She lives on the road, in her Airstream, and I live, you know, here, in Rush Creek." I still have their full attention. "She hadn't even decided if she was going to—"

But I stop, there. Because I don't want my family to start weighing in on Mari's—and my—options. It's not their place and it's not their business, no matter how much they love me and want the best for me. So I just say, "We're still figuring all this out. We need space."

And like I've spoken the magic words, they give us the space we need—literally. They start backing up.

First Easton, with his hands up, palms out. "Of course, dude. Of course."

Then Hanna—surprisingly, falling back to Easton's side, as if taking her cue from him. "I'm sorry, Kane. I didn't mean to—"

"No," I say, quickly. "It's okay. I know you didn't."

Amanda's next. "Kane," she says. "I really stepped in it, huh?" She turns to Mari. "I'm so sorry. I just got so excited, because I really—I'm just sorry. We're—I know we're a lot. I hope—I hope you can forgive me for being such a big mouth."

"You weren't a big mouth," Mari says. "You were just excited. No forgiveness needed." Her voice is surprisingly steady, her chin up. The look of terror has muted somewhat. She's a trouper, for sure. My admiration for her notches up, although it was topline to begin with. But—she hasn't run, she hasn't snapped—unlike me. She hasn't curled up in a ball on the ground whimpering, so in my book, she's a queen.

Amanda follows Easton and Hanna, disappearing around the side of the house.

My mom hangs back. I expect for her to lecture me, but she turns to Mari instead. "Whatever you... whatever you need, I'm here," she tells her. "I'm so excited to be a grandmother again. I would love to have a chance to get to know your baby, but no matter—"

She pauses, her eyes soft on Mari.

Even though we haven't said anything about what's at stake, my mom seems to intuitively grasp how complicated this is. That's my mom for you. Quietly the rock at the center of this family unit. I know it looks like that's Gabe role... and of course he is, too. But underestimate my mom at your peril.

"—no matter what you decide, I'm here for you."

For a long moment, Mari holds my mom's gaze. The two women are almost perfectly still, but it feels like something travels between them. Something in a language I don't know and possibly will never understand.

"Thank you," Mari says, quietly.

My mom touches her on the arm, just a tap, before disappearing around the corner.

I exhale and look up to find Mari looking at the house my family members disappeared to. The panic is gone from her face, and she looks thoughtful.

I don't know what just happened, but maybe this evening isn't the total disaster it seemed like a few minutes ago.

I exhale what feels like a week's worth of breath.

"I'm sorry," Kane tells me. Several times.

"No, it's okay," I say. "They were just being themselves. It's the situation that's messed up. But if you don't mind—I think I might need to head back with Bernadette and hole up."

"Of course I don't mind," he says. "I'll walk you to her, to Bernadette."

We head to the house so I can collect my shoes. I'd kicked them off inside the front door as soon as I'd entered. Lucy and several other women are sitting in the living room, but none of the witnesses to our recent scene are there.

I look around and see only one shoe in the foyer.

"Where's my other shoe?" I ask Kane. The shoes are one of my favorite pairs, Goodwill-acquired, handstitched, red leather Mary Janes.

"Oh, *shit*," I hear from the living room. A moment later, Lucy pokes her head into the foyer. "Are you missing a shoe?" she demands, and then, without waiting for an answer, "Buck! Buck!"

"No," Kane groans. "Buck did *not* eat Mari's shoe."

Lucy frowns. "God, I hope not. One of these days that beast is going to land himself in surgery." She disappears out the front door. Kane and I stand in the foyer in silence, not addressing what just happened outside. The living room has mostly fallen silent, and I can't help feeling like they're listening to us not talking in the front hall, making of it what they will. But maybe I'm just paranoid now—getting outed will do that to you.

My thoughts are in total chaos, a jumble of impressions and feelings, all the big, loving energy of the Wilders and their misperceptions and longings.

For a minute there outside, I wanted to be what they wanted.

But even before Amanda walked around the corner of the house, I was a hot brew of sensations and emotions. And when Kane laid his hand on my belly, my thoughts scattered like dandelion seeds in the wind. It felt so good, better even than his kiss, which makes no sense because that kiss—that kiss was magic. But the belly-touching, that was different—pure and curious and comforting.

When was the last time someone touched me for a reason that wasn't sexual?

I look up. Kane is leaning against the wall, watching me, quietly.

Lucy bursts into the foyer. She has the shoe—somewhat the worse for having caught Buck's interest—in hand. "I'm really sorry, Mari. He's such a menace. I usually tell people not to take off any clothes or shoes when they come in.

We'll replace it—just send me a link and I'll take care of it." I smile at the pleading expression on her face.

"That's not necessary," I respond. "None of my things are so nice that they can't stand a little dog drool."

"That's very kind, really. But please send me a link."

I don't think she's going to accept no for an answer, so I nod.

She turns to Kane. "Do not, under any circumstances, tell Gabe this happened," she says.

Kane squints at her. "Um, why not?"

She crosses her arms. "He reads too much into Buck's behavior."

"What can you read into a dog chewing a shoe?"

Lucy just shakes her head. "It's Gabe," she says, and that seems to be enough for Kane, who lets it drop.

"Would you let everyone know I'm heading out, and say goodbye from me?" I ask Lucy. "I'm feeling kinda wiped out"—I gesture at my built-in excuse.

"Oh, God, yes," Lucy says. "Don't try to make the rounds. It'll take all night, you'll get sucked in again, and you'll never get out of here. I'll tell everyone. Thank you so much for coming—I'm so glad you did."

"Thank you for including me," I say. "I had a good time."

The next thing I know, I'm folded into her hug, my belly between us, and then, just as quickly, she releases me.

Kane walks silently beside me as I head back to Bernadette. I'm comforted by his presence, even though he doesn't say anything. When we get to the RV, he opens the driver's side door for me and helps me up—a hand on my back. It's another touch with no purpose but to show caring

—and for some reason, I tingle like a fourth of July sparkler.

"Thank you."

"Fingers and toes accounted for?"

I nod. "Sleep tight." And he shuts the door.

As I drive back to Kane's place, they're all in my head. Hanna and her bluntness. Easton and his surprising gentleness. Amanda and her enormous heart. Lucy and her generously offered friendship. Barb Wilder and her unconditional love.

Kane and his—well, everything. Washcloth and cooing and peekaboo and disgusting diaper change and quick leap to my defense and obvious intense affection for his friends and family.

He's such a good man. He has such a good family.

And even if the Wilders, if Rush Creek, are not what I want for myself?

They're what I want for my baby.

I know what I need to do.

24

KANE

I don't stay long at the party—just another few minutes to say my goodbyes.

When I get home, I slide out of the car and walk toward Mari's Airstream. It's not a fully conscious decision. I just know I need to check on her again, make sure she's okay after all that—Wilder-ness.

I knock, quietly, in case she's conked out sleeping already.

I hear her feet shuffling behind the door, and she answers in her pajamas—a pair of joggers that can't possibly stretch another inch and a navy long-sleeved t-shirt that no longer quite reaches her waistband. Her feet are bare and her hair is down. She looks young and vulnerable. If I didn't know that she was so strong, I sure wouldn't guess it now.

"Hey." She steps back to let me in. "I'm glad you're here."

The stairs aren't unfolded, so I take a huge step up to her, closing the door behind me.

She cocks her head. "Can I get you something? Tea? Orange juice? I think I have an old bottle of bourbon somewhere?"

I laugh. "No. I'm good. I just wanted to make sure you're okay. That was so much. So much Wilder energy. *I* was overwhelmed, and I've known them my whole life."

She shakes her head. "They're good people. Really good people."

"They are—just *a lot*."

She's facing me, but she's looking past me, at something in the distance. "Kane," she says.

"What?"

"I still don't know what I want for myself. Not exactly. But if you—if you want to be—" She presses her mouth into a tight line, tries again. "If you want to raise the baby—"

I don't know yet whether she means by myself or together, and that question will keep me up nights till it's answered, but this is a huge step forward for us. For the baby. For me.

"God! Yes!"

She smiles, slow and almost shy. "Then you should. I want that. I want the baby to grow up with a supportive father and a supportive extended family. I want this for both of you."

I'm feeling so much at once, I don't know what to do with it. I settle on reaching out a hand.

"May I?"

She nods, then takes my hand and guides it to where her belly bulges, life moving—fierce, determined—under the surface.

"Hello, baby," I say. "Is it weird if I talk to your belly?"

She shakes her head.

"I'm gonna be your daddy," I tell the small person inside there. "I love you already."

Mari makes a small sound. I look up. She's biting down so hard on her lip that it must hurt.

"You okay?" I ask her.

"Yeah," she says. "It's just—that makes it real. I was trying not to—not to let it be real. So it wouldn't be so hard."

"I didn't think about that," I say. "I'll stop."

"No," she says. "Don't stop. It's nice."

We're both quiet for a moment, her hand still on mine.

"I'm gonna hug your mom now," I tell her belly. "Because she just gave me the most amazing gift. Also," I say, trying to lighten the moment, "she staved off no end of lengthy lawsuits and complicated custody battles."

She's laughing. "Thank you for not saying all that *beforehand*."

"It was very restrained of me, don't you think?" I raise an eyebrow. I am not really sure I would have gone to battle with her, involved lawyers and the courts, but I can't deny it was a possibility.

"So restrained."

"C'mere, you," I tell her, and she does, sliding easily into my arms. The lemon smell of her comes, too, and the warmth of her body, the softness of her curves, the feel of her arms around me. My body wakes up instantly, and if it weren't for her belly, keeping us at a safe distance, I'd—

I draw back before I can fully form the thought, before I can picture what I want.

Instead I ask, "So you won't pursue adoption."

"Right," she says.

"Does this mean..." I hesitate, wanting to tread carefully. Knowing for sure I'll raise my baby is enormous, but it's not the only thing I want. "Does this mean you're thinking about staying?"

She tilts her head. "I don't know."

It's not a no. Which right now feels pretty damn good. "You don't have to know the answer yet."

"Thank you. I don't think a lot of men would be as awesome about this as you're being."

I polish my knuckles on my chest and make her laugh.

"When did you know you were okay with me raising the baby?" I ask her.

"As soon as I found you, saw you again, I thought it might be the right answer. So that was before the breakfasts and the Boston cream pie. And your family—they really are kind of..."

"Like a love bomb?"

She laughs again, which makes my chest fill up with light.

"I can tell if the baby grows up here, it'll always be with people who love it. You're amazing with other kids, you'll be amazing with your own. And there are so many people who will support both of you."

"And you, if you stay."

"Well," she says. "I'm not—ruling it out."

"Good," I say. "Because hear this. I like you, Marigold Barrymore, and I'm asking you to seriously think about staying here and raising this baby together. Or at least treating Rush Creek as your permanent home base. You could travel. There are tons of families where one parent is on the road for work."

Her eyes are big and soft, like they were when our hands met over her belly. Like they were when my family swept over her like a tidal wave. Like they were during that long quiet moment of affection and understanding between Mari and my mother.

Big, soft, and vulnerable, and the fissure in my chest opens into a spiderweb of holes and cracks.

She bites her lip again, her gaze skidding nervously around Bernadette's interior. I think the word *families* was too much for her. "Don't freak out," I say, hoping I come across as gentle, echoing her words to me from the first day she arrived in Rush Creek.

That totally makes her smile. "I'm not freaking out. I just don't want you to get your hopes up."

"I'm a big boy. I can handle it."

Her eyes settle on my face, and she studies me. It's a strange feeling. Good, I think—but foreign. I'm not sure anyone in my family really *looks* at me. Not like this, like she's trying to read all the meanings behind my words.

"Okay," she says, finally. "I will seriously think about staying. But *no promises*."

It's better than nothing. And I won't give up. Not yet.

"I still have a lot of tricks up my sleeve," I say, as much to myself as to her. "I still haven't made you my bacon-and-tomato strata for breakfast."

A little half-moan escapes her mouth—and lodges itself at the base of my spine.

"And, sweetheart, I give a mean foot massage."

The next sound out of her mouth is a full-throated

moan, and it's my turn to stifle a groan. My own damn fault for calling off the kissing. A little kissing would go down super smoothly right about now.

I'm staring at her mouth. I force myself to stop.

"And now I know how to make Boston cream pie," I remind her. "That's a life skill."

She bursts out laughing. "Again, no promises," she says, sternly, but I've made her laugh, and that feels like the biggest win of all.

There's never been anything I wanted this much. I'll fight for it.

Even though I'm the boy next door, I'm also a Wilder. And Wilders don't back down when something matters to them.

25

———————

KANE

When I stumble out my front door Monday morning, to start our road trip to Salt Lake City, the last thing I expect to see is Mari, bright-eyed and wide awake, standing on a step stool and cleaning Bernadette's windshield.

I don't want to startle her, so I don't call out. Instead I approach slowly, and when she turns and smiles at me, I say, "Are you sure that's safe?"

"I'm being super careful, I promise," she says.

"You're—awake."

"I know, right? I get so excited for trips. I couldn't sleep anymore."

She hops off the ladder like a little bird, beaming. Despite days of evidence that she's not a morning person, she's dressed, bouncing on her toes, and obviously raring to go—at 6 a.m.

"Breakfast is donuts today," I say, opening the box I procured the night before, and handing her one.

"Boston cream," she breathes, and all of a sudden I'm wide awake, too, six a.m. or no.

"It's not really Boston cream," I warn. "It's weak fake custard."

"Oh, now he's all *I make real Boston cream*," she teases. "Feeling pretty good about yourself, Mr. Baker, huh?"

"I'm just saying. That donut is not the real thing."

She dips her tongue into the dimple on the side of the donut and swipes up the cream. "Mmm." Her eyes meet mine, and mine betray me, telling her exactly what I think about all of that—dimple, cream, tongue, and humming sound I can feel the whole length of my cock.

A mischievous smile spreads over her face, and that—I don't know what to do with that. I don't know what to do with that Mari at all—all pixie and excitement and tease, just like she was the first night we met, when I was helpless.

I turn away, quickly making myself busy loading my stuff. Bernadette is pulling a trailer that will eventually contain the red range Mari spec'd for Christian Grey's Airstream. Right now it contains my duffle and a few camping supplies. As long as we make good time, we'll camp only one night, near Salt Lake.

Out of deference to Mari, and because I trust myself exactly as far as I can throw Clark, I have my own tent, sleeping bag, and sleeping pad.

The donut dimple only reconfirms this decision.

When I sidle up to Bernadette's driver's side door, Mari slides between me and her RV. "I'll take first shift," she says. "I'm gonna have to stop to pee every thirty seconds, anyway, so we can do shortish shifts."

Her logic makes sense. I don't fight her.

She swings herself up into the driver's seat, agile still for someone who's closing in on eight months pregnant.

As soon as I climb up next to her she starts Bernadette, lets her warm up a sec, and maneuvers her out of my driveway with surprising ease.

"Want me to map the route?" I ask, pulling out my phone.

"No need," she says, with a little shrug. "I know how to get there. We'll do 20 to 84 to 21."

"When you say you know how to get there—did you Google Maps that?"

She shakes her head.

"So are you *sure*?"

She rolls her eyes in my direction. "Of course, I'm sure. If there's one thing I know, it's the roads in this country."

"Wait a second," I say. "You're doing all that out of your head?"

She nods. "Yeah. My mom used to have me navigate. I spent my whole childhood studying maps and looking at route apps. I know how many hours it takes to drive between pretty much all U.S. cities and most landmarks that anyone cares about."

"Wall Drug to the north entrance of Yellowstone."

She shrugs. "About eight. That's not even tough."

I pull out my phone, and... she's right. I think for a moment. "Canyon de Chelly to Iowa City."

"Twenty hours?" she hazards, with a tilt of her head.

Google confirms her guess to within an hour. "Wow. That's impressive."

She scrunches up her nose. "Nah," she says. "That's not even a hard one. Trying to think of one that would really be a challenge. Like... Disney World to Glacier. No one ever puts those two on the same trip, and there's no really straightforward way to do it. It's like, 75, 24, 57—oh what the hell is the one that gets you from 57 to 70. 64? And a few after that but I get foggy. I'm thinking forty hours."

"That's amazing," I say, pulling up the route.

"Nah. You get good at whatever you do over and over again, right? I've got way more than ten thousand hours of navigating the U.S. on my mom's whims, and my own."

For shits and giggles, I Google our route anyway.

"Wait," I say. "The route you just said, the one you're taking us on, that doesn't take us to Salt Lake City. It takes us to *Idaho City.* Not the same thing at all."

"Yeah, no, I know," she says. "It's a little detour. I want you to see a couple of things I think you'll appreciate."

"What things?"

"Things." She's beaming again, bouncing in her seat, full of life and waking my body up like her blood is rushing through my veins. Or maybe that's just the sight of her gorgeous tits jiggling under her cute top—pale pink, clinging to the soft globes of her breasts, and flowing out over her belly.

"C'mon, you can tell me."

She shakes her head. "Nope. I want it to be a surprise." Another little bounce on the seat, another surge of blood into my groin. At least tonight I'll be sleeping alone in a tent, where, if quiet, I can do what needs to be done.

"How out of our way are we going?"

She shrugs. "A little."

"But then we won't make it to Salt Lake today."

Her smile gets bigger. "Is that a problem?"

I told Gabe I'd be back late tomorrow, ready to pick up work again on Wednesday morning. I'm feeling extra guilty because I never turned over my new snow adventure plan to him, the one Hanna and I were supposed to develop before I left on this trip. He gave me some Gabe-glare about it, but he didn't lower the boom. I think he was trying to cut me some well-deserved slack. Unlike my brothers—especially Brody and Easton—I never have to be hounded or ridden or reminded—and I *never* flake out on being where I'm supposed to be.

Of course, that was before, before I picked up a woman in a Vegas bar, had sex with her, and got her pregnant. It was before I signed up to be a dad, before I decided that everything I'd ever had paled in comparison to what I wanted.

And what I want right now? Doesn't include hurrying back to Rush Creek to be Gabe's easy-going little brother and most reliable worker.

I take a deep breath. "No," I say. "Whatever you want to show me, I want to see it."

I even manage to not make it sound dirty.

"A COWBOY really might amble into the street for a showdown here," I observe.

It's early afternoon and after several bathroom breaks and sandwiches eaten on the go, we've just turned onto Idaho City's main drag.

"There!" she says. "Pull in over there."

I ease Bernadette into the lot she's pointing out, then

into a space that's really not big enough for us—but beggars can't be choosers. When I cut the engine and finally look up, I see—

"Holy shit!"

"Right?" she says, bouncing in her seat with excitement.

"That's—"

Actually I'm not sure what the right adjective is. On one hand, the business in front of me most closely resembles a trash heap. It looks like it should have been condemned years ago. A big plank out front has been spray-painted with the business name. *The Sluice Box*. Most of the front door is covered with a giant stop sign. In fact, the whole property is plastered with signs. Budweiser. Blatz. Idaho City. There are gas pumps out front. A section of weathered picket fence. A wagon wheel, an old-fashioned plow, an ancient table, a broken-down bench. Up top, the store's original architecture has been embellished with an ancient windmill and a garret that doesn't belong—among a host of other things.

It's—ugly and beautiful.

"It's fantastic." My voice is surprisingly husky—because I'm weirdly, oddly, moved that she knew exactly how much I would love this. I look over at her, and she's smiling back, a small, secret, victorious smile. My hand almost goes out to stroke a few wild strands of hair off her forehead, but I pull back at the last minute.

I dig in my bag for my camera instead.

Kicking up dust as we walk, we exit Bernadette and head for the monstrosity.

"Get me some good photos," she says, gesturing at my

Nikon. "I'm going to get us coffees. Decaf for me," she clarifies, even though I didn't ask.

I raise my camera. I can't get enough. The signs with their old paint, the cracked wood, and the broken things that someone cared enough about to gather. I could stay here for hours.

She comes back out with two coffees, but doesn't try to hand me mine. She holds onto it while I snap off shot after shot. It's a small thing, but I feel absurdly grateful, and even more so when she unloops my camera bag from over my shoulder and takes that too, leaving my hands and upper body free.

Once I've gotten all the photos I want of the building, I capture incoming visitors, their faces when they first see the Sluice Box, the way they turn to each other, trying to find the right words to express how they feel when they see this collection of things that aren't quite worth saving.

For every photo I take of people, I ask permission and collect names and emails, telling them I make a practice of deleting any people shots I don't have permission for.

"You want me to—?" Mari asks, and when I look at her, she's holding up her phone to ask if I want her to track the names and emails.

"Thank you."

"Of course!"

I don't think she knows what a big deal it is to me, though. I've spent a lifetime grabbing photos in a rush as my family hurried on ahead, eager to get to the big adventure. But not only is she not rushing me, she's encouraging me to take my time. To get what I need.

"Thank you," I say again, and I think she gets it this

time, because her gaze stops on me for a long moment, and then she gives me that same secret pleased smile.

After a while, I stop and drink some of my coffee, surprised to discover it's a latte. "How did you know I drink lattes?"

"You ordered one at the coffee shop. The day we were in town," she says, shrugging.

It's totally foreign to me, this feeling of being seen. Of being…

No, it can't be.

Of being *wooed*.

But she isn't. She wouldn't. I'm the one who wants this. She… wants the road.

She points, and I capture the shot—a purple-haired woman and her Hawaiian-shirted husband, arms full of gilt-edged china cups. They want a copy of the photo, so I air drop it to them once they've set their haul down on the register counter.

"You should look around, too," I tell Mari.

She does, and I grab a string of photos of that, too. She picks objects up and sets them down, expressions flickering so fast over her face that I can't capture them fast enough: puzzlement, wonder, delight. I can feel my face mirroring hers, like it's the only way I can get enough of her.

I take more photos of her than of everyone else combined, and I still don't feel like I've really captured that energy that her skin can't contain.

Mari finds a copy of *Seventeen* magazine from the 1980s, and as we check out, I grab a quick photo of the mustached man explaining to the bored teenager behind the counter why the incomprehensible piece of electronic music equipment in his husband's arms is the answer to, if not prayers, then at least months of searching.

My coffee's almost cold when we get back in the Airstream.

"Show me," she says, gesturing at the Nikon.

I do, paging through the photos, holding the camera out so we can both see the screen. My attention roams between the photos and her face—a smile, eyes widening, mouth opening. She bites her lip at a photo of her, touching a doll's cheek.

"You made me look so pretty," she says.

My chest hurts.

"You are so pretty," I say. "You're fucking beautiful. If our baby is half as beautiful as you are—"

I stop. I went too far, and when my eyes find her, she's frozen.

"I'm sorry," I say.

"No," she says quietly. "It's—it's all right."

She hands me back the camera, and I take it, my throat tight.

"Those are really fucking amazing," she says. "You're— really fucking amazing."

The tightness spreads into my chest, and it has sharp edges that are part pleasure, part pain.

The moment stretches. Then she puts her hands on the wheel, like she's decided something, and her whole energy shifts, like she's put on a different skin.

"You ready?" she asks. "Ready for our next adventure?" She turns and smiles at me, just a little too big to be real. Even so, the smile loosens the tightness in my throat.

"Definitely," I tell her.

26

MARI

Traveling with Kane is a revelation. The best possible kind.

This morning, after we hit the road, he messed with the radio every ten minutes, never satisfied with what he found. I gave him shit about it, because I'll listen to anything. After a while, though, I kind of liked it, the way he jumped around. His restlessness about music didn't quite fit with who I thought he was—but it also did.

I think Kane Wilder wants a lot more than he lets himself want. I think he's put himself in a nice, neat, well-behaved package because his brothers stole all the thunder. But I don't think this well-behaved package is who he really is.

I think I'm seeing who he really is now.

He insisted on buying me lunch and checked in about whether I wanted to avoid cold cuts (because some docs say to skip them during pregnancy). When I asked how he knew that, he said he'd bought a pregnancy book, which he was reading. But he also said he didn't want me to feel like he was policing me. He said he respected whatever I decided about how to take care of myself and the baby.

He never complained about how many times we had to stop for the bathroom. He offered to change places with me frequently, but he didn't get all alpha and paternalistic with me when I said I wanted to keep driving. He just said, "Tell me when you need a break."

I knew how much he'd love the Sluice Box—but I didn't predict how much I'd love watching him there, capturing everything with his camera. I kept trying to guess what he'd shoot next, and a lot of times I was right. He likes anything unusual, anything that surprises him. He likes people's faces when they're animated, or full of emotion. He likes bits of landscape that don't look like much till you get them from just the right angle. He likes things that don't quite belong.

And he likes me. He took a lot of photos of me. And I loved seeing myself through his eyes. Not just bright hair and freckles and green eyes, not just my outsized boobs and round tummy. But those photos made me glow. They made me fascinating. They made my body tingle as if he'd outlined my lips and cheekbones and collarbones with knowing fingertips, instead of just capturing them as images.

And then he said that thing. *You're so pretty. You're fucking beautiful. If our baby is half as beautiful as you are—*

And I hoped it, too. I could see it, for the first time—our baby, swaddled tight, capped with bright red hair, and Kane gazing down with awe in his eyes.

I made myself focus on the road until the vision slid away.

WE PULL up to Black Magic Canyon late in the afternoon. Kane looks around, puzzled. "This is your big reveal?"

"Hold on. Be patient."

I understand his confusion. All we can see right now is acres of Idaho rangeland—grass and brush and an unusually large amount of dust for late March because it's been so dry. In the far distances, mountains rise, jagged and beautiful—but right here?

Not impressive.

Until we follow the path down into the canyon. Then Kane opens his mouth and turns to me with an expression I'm coming to love. Like I've given him an unexpected gift.

"It's like another planet," he says, his voice awed.

He turns in a circle, taking in our surroundings. Black Magic Canyon was formed when the Big Wood River carved into lava flows—tens of thousands of years ago. In some places, walls rise up fifty feet.

He reaches out and touches the basalt. Strokes it. There's a bed of shale beneath our feet, and rocks strewn everywhere, with most of the canyon rock being a striking jet black. Over time it's been carved into curves and curls, slickly smooth in places. It's tactilely delicious, as well as a feast for the eyes. His, when he looks up at me, are big and earnest.

"I love it. Thank you."

Kane says thank you a lot. Part of it is good, boy-next-door manners, but part is sheer, straight-up gratitude, which does something messy to me, because like I said, I don't think he gets what he wants, anything tailored to his interests and not his brothers', very often. And I think I can hear the difference in his voice when something's real to him. When it's a thank-you from the soul.

His camera comes out, and he shoots as we walk, making me stop every few yards. Sometimes he pins me into the frame of his photo, too, and every time I can feel his eyes on me. Now that I know more about what he sees when he looks at the camera screen, my skin tingles, the way it did when I looked at his photos earlier.

"Look at this." He kneels and sets a hand into a swirl of rock, sweeps his touch over it.

I start laughing. Because...

"What? What?"

I show him. The way the rock curls and folds. Like a Georgia O'Keefe flower. Like a pussy. Clit, inner and outer lips. He starts laughing, too, but he doesn't take his hand off it. He gives the smooth rock another stroke, looking straight at me, locking my gaze into his. Just, idly. Super casual. His thumb sliding up over the nub of rock where the folds come together.

My own laughter has dried up with all the saliva in my mouth.

Kane Wilder can smirk when he wants to, and it's really fucking hot.

27

———————

KANE

I wake up in the middle of the night soaking wet. In a puddle.

"Shit," I say. "Shit, shit, *shit.*"

I left the rain fly off, which makes me a fucking idiot. I can feel Clark's fury from hundreds of miles away.

This part of Idaho has less than a 25 percent chance of rain on any given day in March, I tell imaginary Pissed-off Clark. *And the percentage drops as the month goes on. There wasn't any in the forecast.*

Tell that to your hypothermia, Pissed-off Clark flings back.

I crawl out of the tent. Water runs down my face.

Most of my stuff is still in the trailer we're hauling behind Bernadette. I could climb in there. But it's not heated, my sleeping bag is soaked, and I didn't bring as much wool and fleece as I should have, because this was never supposed to be a wilderness trip.

It's not so cold out that I'm in any danger of actually dying, I tell Pissed-off Clark.

You don't know you're hypothermic when you're hypothermic, Pissed-off Clark slings back.

God damn it. Pissed-off Clark is not going to let me stay here in the rain or sleep in a trailer when there's warm, dry shelter just a hundred feet away.

And he's right, and I know it.

I drag my sorry ass up to Bernadette's door and knock. Quietly, in case Mari's asleep. I guess I'm sort of hoping she is. If she doesn't answer, I won't have to go in there, and if I don't go in there, I won't give in to temptation.

To kiss her. To touch her, a slow, leisurely exploration of her body with my hands and mouth, until she's begging me to fuck her.

And then...

Because I'm all out of self-control. I'm all out of the energy I'd need to remind myself of reasons I can't touch her.

The door swings open, and she's standing there, blinking at me sleepily. Alarm rushes over her face, and then amusement, and then—curiosity, I think. Her gaze runs over me. All of me—the water running down my face, my wet half-zip base layer, the wet sweats I pulled on over my bottom base layer, because it gave me a thin extra layer of armor. Which is basically useless, because despite the chilling cold, I'm sporting yet another semi, and I swear her eyes snag on it on their way back up to my face. Her cheeks go pink, which doesn't help the situation.

"Get in here," she orders, which also doesn't help.

I obey, because...

I wish I could blame it on Pissed-off Clark, but I know

the truth. The truth is that I want to go inside, and I want... her.

"I'm sorry," I say, taking a step toward her. "Clark would have my head on a platter. I fucked up with the rain fly and woke up drenched."

"Just come in," she says. "Clark's not here, and I don't judge."

As I step inside she grabs a towel and hands it to me, and I do my best to dry myself off. I try to keep my arm or the towel in front of my wet, clinging clothes. Because my semi isn't becoming any more semi.

She eyes me. "Give me that," she says, holding a hand out for the towel.

When I don't give it over, she snatches it. "Lean down," she says.

I do, and she towels off my hair. Her breasts are inches from my head. I'm looking down at her belly, full of our baby. Even through the towel, her touch feels blissful.

Then she hands me the towel and I arrange it discreetly in front of my groin.

She marches back toward the bedroom area and returns with a small stack of clothes. "I don't know if anything will fit you."

I hold up what are obviously her biggest clothes and laugh out loud. Her mouth turns up slowly.

"Yeah," she says. "Not so much. What do we do?" She wrinkles her eyebrows. "Okay. Here's the plan. I'll make up the lounge for you with sheets and blankets. Then I'll get in bed. And then you get undressed and towel off and get in bed. Make sure you wring out your clothes and spread them out so they have the best chance of being dry in the morning."

She wants me to sleep *naked*. In her Airstream. Or maybe I should say she wants me to 'sleep' naked because there is no way I am going to be able to fall asleep naked six feet away from her.

And there's also no way I'm going to be able to engage in the one activity that might help me sleep.

But unless I want to be soaked to the bone all night, this is my best bet. So I take the sheets and blankets from her arms and make up the convertible lounge myself.

She slips to the back of Bernadette, and I hear the sounds of her getting comfortable in bed again.

I wish the invitation had been to climb in there with her.

Instead, I use the already wet towels to wring out my clothes, then drape all the wet things over the dinette. Then I climb under the covers—naked—on the lounge bed. It's not the most comfortable sleeping surface in the world. In fact, it might be one of the most uncomfortable. But it hardly matters since there's no way I'll sleep.

I stare at the metal ceiling, at a light fixture that looks like an original, trying not to think about Mari, six feet away.

"Kane." Her voice comes from Bernadette's bedroom end.

"Yeah?"

"You settled?"

"Yeah." Except for the fact that I can't stop noticing the cool caress of the sheet on my dick, no matter how I turn, no matter how I move. Every time it scrapes like a tease over the head, my cock throbs and jumps, which makes it worse.

And her voice, sleepy and confidential, isn't helping.

"I looked at the photos you posted on your Insta. I love the one of the woman watching her kid climb on the rocks in the canyon. She looks terrified and proud at the same time."

"Thanks." I'd liked that one a lot, too.

"You *see* people. It's a gift. I see you hanging back with your family, too, watching them, taking in everything."

I rake a hand through my hair. "Yeah, well... maybe it's a gift. I'm not always sure."

"What do you mean?" Her voice is barely more than a murmur, but it carries through the echoey inside of our aluminum cave.

"I mean..." I think of the other day, when my mom fretted that I'd forgotten to take my own pizza order. "Sometimes they forget I'm there. Sometimes... *I* forget I'm there."

"I can see that." Not judgy. Just: hearing me. Just like she sees me. "They all have their roles. Gabe's the boss. I'm guessing Brody's the bad boy, or at least he dresses the part?"

I nod. "Close enough."

"Clark's—what?"

"Forest warrior. Easton's the panty-melter."

She laughs at that. "Right, I got that feeling, distinctly."

"In your panties?" I tease, over a rising twinge of jealousy.

"Ha, no. He's too slick for me."

"That's what they all say. Right before their panties go up in flames."

She chuckles. "So, boss, bad boy, forest warrior, panty-melter. And Amanda's the girl."

"Right."

She's quiet for a moment. Then she says, "And you?"

"I've always been... the boy next door. The peacemaker. The fixer."

The covers rustle in the back. "Do you remember when you first knew that was your job? Brody's probably the bad boy because he got stuck chasing Gabe's shadow. And Amanda's the girl because she is. Easton's the youngest, so I'm guessing that plays a pretty big role in him figuring out how to be the charmer. But you?"

"Yeah," I say. "I remember."

I close my eyes.

"It was pretty soon after my dad died. My mom was diagnosed with breast cancer. Which was—I mean, you can imagine. Your dad dies and then, blam, your mom has cancer."

"Kane," she whispers.

"Everyone was falling apart. My mom was in chemo, and she was just—I mean, you know. She was barely hanging in, and my brothers were all causing a ton of trouble. There was this one night when everyone was being a dick and giving my mom shit, and at some point I joined in, too. She gave me this super sad look and said, 'Not you, too.'"

She makes a small *oof* noise.

"Afterwards I apologized to her, and she said, 'There are

too many wild men in this family, Kane. Just be our good boy.'"

She's quiet in the back. Then she says, "That's a lot to live up to. For a teenage boy. You took it all on, didn't you?"

I'd never really thought about it that way before, but in this moment, I know she's right.

"You've got an artist's soul. And all those mountain men brothers. Big, physical, rowdy. Must have been hard sometimes."

My chest aches and my throat's tight again. I try to speak, but I can't.

"You okay?" she asks.

Air finds its way out again with a little huff. "Yeah. I mean I love the shit out of them. You know I do."

"I know."

"But, yeah. Maybe. What you said." I take a breath. "Can I tell you something?"

"Mmm-hmm."

"In Vegas. My brothers liquored me up and dared me to pick up a stranger, and when I said I couldn't, they said, sure you can. Just pretend you're Easton. So that's what I was doing that night. That's how I got up the nerve to talk to you. That's who I was pretending to be when we..."

It's all there—her scent, the feel of her body beneath mine, her cries of pleasure. I slide a hand down my abs to cup my balls.

"It wasn't fair to you, me pretending to be someone I wasn't. I guess I just wanted to say that."

I listen, craning my ears—my whole body really—for her reaction.

I can hear the rain pounding on the aluminum roof of

the RV. I can hear it landing with soft definite drops in a bucket or bowl somewhere within Bernadette's curved shell—I remember her mentioning that Bernadette could use more waterproofing. I listen, and I wait.

"Kane," she murmurs. Just the sound of it is enough to send sensation sliding through my chest, down into my dick. "That night. It was really you. And it was really me." I hear her gather her breath. "You can't fake... what we did."

I close my eyes, seeing it. Feeling it. Her words unknot something in me. She's right: Fundamentally, wholly—I was myself with her that night. Maybe more myself than I'd been in a long time.

I am so myself right now that I can't contain it all inside my skin. It needs to go somewhere. I can hear a clock ticking, or maybe it's Bernadette's exoskeleton settling. I try to ignore the tease of the sheet against my dick, which is nothing compared to the heat building from inside me, heat she's stoked with her words. Heat and pressure, and that's what I blame for the words that jump out of me:

"It was good, wasn't it?"

"It was so good."

Her voice is a teasing rasp.

I can hear the shifting of her covers, of her body in the other room. My mind goes bananas with imagining things. She *isn't*. She can't be.

God, I hope she is.

"What did you like about it?"

The question drops from my lips.

I've definitely gone too far. I hold my breath, waiting for her to remind me of my own rules. Of our good reasons to keep sex out of this. My cock jumps against the sheet; I wrap my fist around it and squeeze. The pressure is a relief, but it also amps me up a level.

"Oh, *God*, everything," she says roughly, and against my palm, I get harder. "Your hands on my wrists, your body pressing me against the wall, your mouth—God, your mouth, Kane. I couldn't stop thinking about it—for weeks. Months. I tried to hook up with a couple of guys in those months, but I always quit after the first kiss, because it wasn't you kissing me. That sounds nuts, right? I'm nuts for saying that. It was *one night*."

"You're not nuts," I say, thinking of Veronica and the bland kissing, the bland sex. No wonder she dumped me. If I was more myself than I'd ever been with Mari, I was an empty shell with Veronica, not even letting myself think about what I was missing. "It was a hell of a night."

"You know what I liked best?" Mari whispers.

I'm stroking myself now, and I want to know. I *need* to know. If she is, too. "Are you...?" I rasp out.

"Am I what?" Her voice is husky, teasing.

"Are you touching yourself?"

It's barely above a whisper, but the words feel huge and loud in the six feet between us. I glide a hand up over the head of my cock, picking up the slickness, spreading it over myself. Wishing it were hers, her slickness on my fingers, her body under my hand.

"If I said I were? Would that be breaking the rules?" I can hear the smile in her voice.

I shake my head, but of course she can't see me. "No. God no." My hand is flat now, the meat of my palm applying perfect pressure to my cock. My balls are drawn up. God, that happened fast, and I want more time, I don't want this to end too soon. But I can't stop the slow rocking motion that's winding pleasure up from the deepest part of me.

"No. It wouldn't count. It would just be you getting yourself off before you fall asleep."

"And you?"

My voice is huskier than hers. "And me getting myself off, before I sleep. We wouldn't even tell each other we were doing it."

"Kane." It's almost a moan this time. "You have no idea. How horny being pregnant makes me. It's because there's all this extra blood flow everywhere. I'm all swollen and... and *needy*," she says.

"Jesus. Jesus, Mari." My voice is cracked and raw in the dark. I clamp my hand tight around the base of my cock, staving off release. Not. Yet. I want more. More of this feeling, more of her confiding, teasing voice in the dark. "How horny?"

"I make myself come at least once a day. Twice some days."

I groan. I can't help it. "And what do you think about when you're doing that?"

"You." This time, unmistakably, it's a moan.

"Mari." Halfway between a grunt and a groan. My fist is working now, slick with precum.

"I think about how you—ah, Kane, God—I think about how you wouldn't come until I did. And the tightness in your face, like you were just barely holding on. All that restraint, all that self-control, for a woman you didn't even know and would probably never see again... and I just thought, what would it be like to be with a guy like that, who cared that much, who gave that hard—"

Then she's calling out my name, and making small, wordless, whimpering cries, and, "I'm coming, Kane, and it's all for you."

I'm coming too, thick, gripping, mean spasms that feel like they're rising up from the very bottom of me. It's all for her. All of it.

"Me too," I say. Because that's all I can manage.

28

KANE

After I clean up, I sleep. Deeply.

And when I wake up, Mari is cooking eggs a couple of feet from my head.

"Hey," I say.

"Hey."

She smiles at me. A big, warm, *oh my God that was good* smile, and it lights me up from the inside.

"You, um, sleep well?" I raise both my eyebrows.

"So well." One corner of her mouth pulls up wryly.

"Any particular reason?"

"I was very relaxed."

"Me too," I tell her.

I'm not nearly so relaxed right now, because *morning*, and because Mari is wearing another shirt that fits like a glove over her beautiful tits, and because I want more. Not just words and my own hand. I'm going to make those words real and bury myself inside her again.

"We're not going to pretend that didn't happen, right?" she says.

"No. Fuck no."

She grins. "Good."

I make a wrap out of my blankets and haul myself out of bed. I come up behind her as she stirs our breakfast and line my body up against hers, so there's only a layer or two of cloth between me and her. I drop a kiss against her neck, and she shivers and wiggles back against my erection. "Mmm," she says. "I *miss* that."

"It misses you, too."

One hand holding the blanket in place, I glide a hand up the side of her body, over her belly, to cup the sweet heavy curve of her breast, my fingers playing with her nipple as it hardens.

"Kane." She's breathless, her hand frozen. "Don't stop."

I have no intention of stopping. None at all. I toy with her nipple more, and she hums her pleasure, wriggling back against me.

But just as I'm about to turn her around and drop my blankets, there's a sound like someone is knocking on the side of the Airstream, and we both jump a foot away from each other.

"Who the hell—?"

"You stir the eggs," she says. "I'm dressed, you're not, I'll get the door."

"I'll get the door," I say. "I have fifty pounds and almost a foot of height on you, we're in the middle of nowhere, and no one knows we're here."

She looks like she wants to protest, but then her eyes drop to her belly, and she concedes the point with a nod.

I grab my long johns, which had been draped over the table, and pull them on. They're still a little damp, unfortunately, but getting the hell startled out of me has done wonders for deflating my erection, so there's that. I yank my sweats on, too.

I approach the door gingerly and peek out through the peephole.

No one's there, but I can still hear the knocking.

"What the—?"

I open the door and look out—and burst out laughing.

"Mari. You have to see this."

She grabs the eggs and sausages off the heat and comes to my side. There's a beautiful red, black, and white woodpecker clinging to the side of the Airstream and tapping the aluminum as if it's going to yield up a bounty of bugs any moment.

"Poor guy," she says. "All the trees in the forest and you had to pick this one. Shoo! No food here!" she slides to the ground, waving her arms at him until he shakes himself, disgruntled with being interrupted at his important work, and flies off into the woods.

"Look at you," she says, as I help her back into Bernadette. "Mmm." She runs a hand over my bare chest, letting her thumb slide along my abs. Her hand slips down to cup the thick ridge growing under my layers of clothes. I counter by bringing my hand back to her stiff nipple, working it until she moans and lifts her mouth for a hot, sweet kiss.

"Do we have time...?" she asks, breaking away.

God, I want to say yes. But the answer's no. "We have to get on the road if we're going to make the appointment with the range guy."

"Damn!" she says. She wriggles, rubbing one thigh

against the other, and I almost lose my willpower—but I also love the idea of her, ready and eager, pressing her thighs together to try to quiet the clamor of—how did she describe it? Oh, right: her swollen, needy pussy.

I grin. It's gonna be a fun day.

Mari serves us both plates of eggs and breakfast sausages, and we sit at the dinette together, eating. It feels right, and comfortable, like it has every morning since she came to Rush Creek, but with an added layer of *knowing* this time. And I don't let myself think about all the things I *don't* know, because I need this. Just like this. For as long as I can have it.

WE SPEND the morning on the road, arriving just before lunchtime. The address lands us at a house that makes The Sluice Box look like a modern palace. A pit bull shepherd barks at us from inside a chain link run. The owner comes down his probably condemned front steps to meet us. He's a refugee from *Mad Max: Fury Road*—clad in coveralls, a ratty white tank top, and a bandana, sporting a frayed and mangy beard.

Every protective instinct I possess is on high alert. I want to sweep Mari off her feet and carry her and the baby to my cave of safety. Which is, technically, Mari's cave of safety, but same diff.

I hang back, though, because if she's been all right for ten years on the road on her own, she doesn't need me to play Neanderthal now.

"It's over this way," he says, and leads us to a beaten-up red Airstream oven.

Mari's mouth gets tight and her eyes squinch up.

"You Photoshopped those photos," she says.

He shrugs.

I'm impressed this guy has the know-how and computer equipment to pull that off. And then irritated at myself for judging his insides based on his outsides.

"You know it's not worth eight hundred," she says, with a shrug. "I'll give you three hundred."

He scoffs. He's big, probably close to my height, and lean but not frail. Mari is tiny compared to him.

Stand down, cave boy next door, I tell myself.

"Five hundred." He crosses his arms and glares at her.

"Three." She glares right back. "Or I walk. You know you're not gonna get more than that."

She shows zero signs of fear. Her body language is big, shoulders broad, arms loose at her sides, feet planted. She looks right at him. And I watch, awed, as his eyes slide away from hers.

"Four," he says.

She shrugs, turns away, and walks towards me. Fearless. I don't think I could turn my back on that guy, but she doesn't even look jumpy.

Mr. Bandana-Head scowls. "You really gonna turn around after coming all this way?"

She shrugs again, not stopping her stroll toward me. "I don't pay money for bad product," she says, and winks at me. *Winks.*

Holy shit, I like this woman.

"Three fifty," he says staunchly, as she draws even with me.

"C'mon Kane." She takes my hand, yanks me gently in the direction of Bernadette. "There's a better one in Moab."

I know for a fact that's not true. Before we left on this trip, we scoured the Internet looking for the right range. They were few and far between, and this one's only competitor was in Eureka Springs, Arkansas.

She puts her hand on the driver's side door handle.

"Okay!" Mr. Bandana-Head calls. "Three!"

Twenty minutes later, Mari has Venmo'd three hundred dollars to Mr. Bandana-Head, the oven is loaded in the trailer, and we're on the road again.

29

MARI

"You love what you do," Kane says, when we're back in Bernadette and headed home. It's his turn to drive.

I'm surprised by the wistfulness in his voice. "Yeah, I do. Don't you?"

"I love skiing. I love my family. But I don't love leading trips. And Gabe wants me to phase out skiing and phase in all this other stuff—igloo camping and snowshoeing."

"In line with the rest of the Wilder vision."

"Right." His voice is glum.

"Could you push back?"

"I could try."

"Could you—maybe this is a terrible question, but could you walk away?"

A muscle tightens in his jaw. "It's a totally reasonable question. But no. If it were just a job, sure. But you've seen them. Wilder Adventures is everything to them. We're everything to each other. When you grow up in a family like that, you don't walk away. We have our own gravitational field. People move to fucking Rush Creek to *become* Wilders."

"You mean, like Lucy and Rachel?"

He frowns. "Yeah."

"That doesn't mean you have to want that. Don't you think they want you to be happy?"

His gaze flicks from the road to me, startled. "Of course they do."

"So if they knew you weren't...?"

"I... don't know."

"It's worth thinking about, right? They love you so much. I know they want what's best for you." I sigh. "I wish I'd grown up like that."

"Do you?"

"With four brothers and a sister and two parents who loved the shit out of me, in a town where everyone has your back? Hell, yeah."

"I thought—I thought you loved the way you grew up."

"No—yes, well... sometimes. There were some amazing things about it. Every day was an adventure. We lived out of an RV. We only stayed in one place for short bursts, so my mom could make money, usually waitressing. In between, we went everywhere. Every national park, every national monument. Every curiosity in every town in every state in the U.S., and the provinces of Canada, too. Sometimes my mom would hook up with a guy and we'd stay a little longer one place."

"Did you like that? When you stayed longer?"

I close my eyes, remembering. "At first. But she inevitably got antsy if we stayed anywhere too long. And when she got antsy, she was miserable, and she'd make me miserable, too."

"That's what you're afraid of. Doing that to your kid."

He says it gently. So gently. And something flares open in the middle of my chest, the fear he's just named. And the grief that sits beside it. They've been in there, waiting for me. My eyes fill with tears.

"Yeah." I dig in my purse for a tissue.

He's quiet, for a moment, then asks, "Do you still talk to her?"

"I didn't hear from her at all for several years, when I was around eighteen. I thought maybe that was it. That she was *done* with me. Then out of the blue she called, and now we have phone or video chats. I've gotten very good at not having any expectations at all from her."

"That sucks," he says, and again, it's so clean and pure and simple, it's like he's dug up a truth I've been holding for too long, and the tears rush into my eyes and throat. It takes me a while this time, before they stop coming, and he doesn't say anything, just keeps driving and letting me cry.

"Does she know you're pregnant? Did you tell her?"

This is a question I really don't want to answer. And I think Kane knows it. His eyes leave the road again, and his gaze is soft for the moment it hovers on me.

"I'm sorry," he says. "I'll shut up now. I'm just—" He presses his lips together. "When it comes to you, I'm incurably curious. I want to know everything about you."

The air in the front cabin seems to still. I thought I never wanted this, to have someone's attention so completely on me, but now that it's here, I never want it to stop. I want him to keep wanting to know me until I've parceled out every last morsel of myself.

And I want that from him, too. I want to see the world through his eyes, through his photos. I want to know why he does the things he does and says the things he says. And I want to help him unwind himself from the tentacles of Wilder love—while he hangs onto the best of it.

Also? I want more of what happened last night. Way more. I want dark, quiet times together in Bernadette, dirty talk, and orgasms that shouldn't be half as good as they are. And next time, I want it to be his hands on me while I come.

Something has happened to me. I've lost control of what I was doing with Kane, what we were doing together. And the worst part is, I can't want it any other way.

"You don't have to answer if you don't want," he says.

"No," I say. "I want to. Yeah, I told her. She said, 'Oh, shit, Mari, I'm sorry.'"

He makes a short, strangled sound.

"Yeah," I agree. "And I hate that she still has the power to hurt me. I hate that it stung so much. She wasn't even trying, and she could still make me feel like a mistake."

His hands are gripping the wheel so tight I can watch his knuckles turning white. And there's a small tic at the corner of his jaw, where the muscle is clenched to within an inch of its life. Somehow, seeing that, seeing his anger, I'm able to exhale a little. Blow out a breath. Take in another one.

"You listen to me." His voice is hard, and rough, and for the first time since Vegas, I can really see the Wilder in him.

Fierce, and strong, the kind of man who will fight for you and yours until there's no fighting left to be done.

"You're not a mistake, Mari," he says. "You're the best decision I've ever made."

I'm not sure what I was doing before, but now I'm crying for real, tears streaming down my face, shoulders shaking with sobs. He finds a place to pull Bernadette over, and he holds me, cradles me, shhhing me quietly, a rush of warm breath past my ear, his arms secure around me.

When I'm finally able to stop crying, I lift my face and he lowers his mouth to mine, kissing me so sweetly and so tenderly that somehow it puts me back together again. Then he pulls away and carefully surveys my face. He pushes a few strands of damp hair off my cheeks and forehead.

My breath catches in my chest at the seriousness of his expression. But before he can say whatever it is that's hovering on his lips, a truck rushes by Bernadette, horn blaring. Kane and I jump as it misses her side mirror by a thousandth of an inch.

"Shit! I'd better get us back on the road," he says. "This shoulder isn't wide enough for us to hang out here."

He maneuvers us carefully back into traffic, and I touch my lips, feeling raw all over, inside and out.

30

KANE

We make good time back to the Boise area.

That intense moment at the side of the road passes, and neither of us makes reference to it again. I don't regret what I said, about Mari being the best decision I ever made. That night in Vegas, and these last three weeks of my life, I've felt more alive than I ever have. I wouldn't give them up for anything. I know what's ahead of me—parenting the baby—isn't going to be easy—and I still don't know if I'll be able to convince Mari to stay. But no matter what, I have no regrets.

I hope she feels the same way.

As we near Boise, Mari tells me that before we settle in at the campground for the night, she has plans for us—of course. We have to sample the local cuisine.

That's how we come to be sitting in Pizza Pie an hour later, a large half habanero, half sausage pie between us.

"You were serious," I say, holding my slice of habanero pizza aloft.

"Dead serious," she says, already several bites into hers. "And I'm serious about potato ice cream, too."

I squint at her. "You cannot be."

"I am."

I bite into my pizza, chew for a minute and... I can feel my whole face going bright red, sweat popping to the surface. I set my slice down.

She grins. "Not your thing, huh."

I shake my head. "Not a spicy food guy."

"That's why I suggested we get half-and-half."

"Good call." I squinted at her. "You gonna go into labor from all those peppers?"

"I think that's a myth," she says. "Spicy food's good for the baby. It'll grow up with a more sophisticated palate if I eat lots of different stuff."

I raise my eyebrow at that. "I think *that's* a myth."

"We can ask her. Later."

"Uh-huh."

I don't miss the fact that Mari said 'her,' but I don't call her on it. I know she saw Lucy's OB/GYN last week, got the (unsurprising) results of the paternity blood draw we'd done shortly after her arrival, and had an ultrasound—but I'm sure she told the doctor and techs she doesn't want to know the baby's sex.

I know I've been thinking of the baby as a *her*, for better or for worse, and wonder if Mari has, too.

I wonder if it means anything if she has.

When we're done with our pizza, she takes me for potato ice cream. Luckily, she's been messing with my head, and potato ice cream isn't actually made from potatoes. It's vanilla ice cream in the shape of a loaded potato. The illusion's so good that I'm a little surprised when my spoon dips smoothly through the cocoa-powder-coated "skin." Between us, we finish the whole thing before returning to the campground.

Once we're parked in our slot, I jump down and head around to the trailer.

"Where are you going?" she demands.

"To get the tent."

She narrows her eyes. "Seriously? You were the one who said we weren't going to pretend that nothing happened."

Yes, but I don't want to assume anything. "That doesn't mean you have to share your sleeping space with me again."

She raises her eyebrows. "Your brothers would."

"Yeah. I'm not my brothers."

"Thank God." She gives me a teasing half-smile that leaves the faint imprint of a dimple in one cheek. "You're way hotter than your brothers. I've studied this question carefully, and I'm a hundred percent sure. Plus, I hear it's supposed to rain again tonight."

"Where'd you hear that?" I've spent the whole day with her, and I don't remember hearing or seeing a forecast at any point.

"My pregnancy hormones told me." Her voice is smoky.

Oh. "I like your pregnancy hormones."

She crooks a finger, beckoning me back toward Bernadette's side door. "C'mon, Hot Wilder."

I follow her inside. She plops down on the lounge and kicks off her shoes, groaning. "We weren't even on our feet much and my feet are killing me," she says. "I believe you mentioned something about convincing me to stay in Rush Creek by promising me foot massages?" She wriggles her toes against Bernadette's carpeted floor and tosses me a naughty sideways smile.

It should be just my libido that's jumping for joy, but there's something else, a warmth in my chest that I can't deny.

I sit down on the other end of the lounge and reach for her feet, drawing them into my lap. She's wearing a long banana-yellow flowy tent of a dress and a pair of socks with purple cartoon octopi on them. I tug a sock off and wrap my hand around her foot, gently massaging.

She moans. "God, Kane. You could do that professionally."

"I mean, it would be a natural fit with leading ski trips," I point out, ignoring the effect of her moan on my body. Her foot is just a couple of inches from the affected body part, but I focus on finding the tender points and easing my thumb into the muscle.

"Kane..." she moans again.

She looks up, catches my dark look, and giggles. "What?" she says innocently. "It feels really good."

"Just you wait," I say. "I have many talents."

"I knooooow." The smoke is back in her voice, a tease I feel everywhere.

I raise my eyebrows. "You want me to cut the foot massage short?"

"No! No. Keep going. I'll be good."

There's a pillow behind her, and as I touch her, I watch her whole body melt into it. She leans back and closes her eyes in bliss. And God, she's pretty, her face slack with pleasure, color in her cheeks. Her nipples visible, just a hint, through the fabric of her dress and bra.

I alternate between feet until she's just a puddle on the pillow, relaxed under my touch, and then I slowly expand my exploration to her ankles. My caress is lighter now, just the whisper of fingers, and she whole-body shivers. The next stroke connects her ankle to the inside of her knee, and she huffs out a breath, arching her back just enough to show me more of her nipples under her dress. Holy crap. She's so responsive.

"Kane," she whispers.

"Yeah, babe?"

"That feels so, so good."

I drag my fingertips up her satiny soft inner thigh, stopping just before the edge of her panties, and she tries to slide to meet my touch. I hold her down with two hands on her hips, and she bucks up, a whimper on her lips.

"Not yet."

Now my mouth is on the inside of her ankle. The skin there is baby soft. I trail kisses up her inner leg, and down again, teasing.

This is messing me up, too. Like, a lot. Because with my mouth on the inside of her thigh, I can smell her arousal, rich and salty, calling to me. And when I sit up to assess her, her face is flushed bright, her eyes unfocused, her lower lip slack. Her nipples are tight buds now. I reach up, cup her breast, and find that peak with my thumb, brushing slowly —so slowly—back and forth across the cloth, until she makes a needy, broken sound.

Her hips are tilting and reaching, and I don't even think she knows it.

"Turn this way," I tell her, guiding her so she's facing out. Then I kneel between her legs. Coaxing her to lift up so I can get her panties free, tugging them down.

She's a whimpering, wet mess, and I love it.

I part her gently and kiss her clit, and she bucks her hips.

"Hold still."

"I can't," she says.

"You can." But just to make sure, I grip her hips and bury my face, pinning her in place while I lick her. She tastes even better than she smells, and my own self-control feels like a thin and fraying thread.

"I need—"

"What do you need?"

"Your fingers. In me."

"Jesus," I say roughly, and give them to her, deep and crooked up to find her G spot, and when I bend down to suck again, she comes, clenching around my fingers and crying out.

I ease back up on the lounge, to see her panting and limp.

31

MARI

It takes me a while to catch my breath and sit up.

Kane makes me come harder than anyone ever has, and I don't think it's even a technique thing. It's a *Kane* thing. It's his self-assurance and thoughtfulness—all the time, not just when we're physically intimate—and the fact that for some reason I can't completely fathom, I feel safe in his arms. In his care.

"That felt so good," I tell him.

He grins, self-satisfied, which is a great look on him. The boy next door with a little sex-induced cockiness is even better than an alpha guy who thinks he's the shit and doesn't need to be grateful for what he gets.

It's my turn to slide to the floor and kneel.

"Mari."

His voice is rough, already a plea. And I understand why when I go to unbutton him. He's harder than steel behind his zipper. When I free him, his cock bounds up to meet me, long and thick and greedy. His balls are already drawn up, and that's hot, too—he was getting off on giving me head. I take him in my mouth, and for some reason all I can think about is what he said earlier. *You're the best decision I ever made.* I've never been that for anyone, not ever.

So, yeah, I want to make him come like I just came, to make him feel as good as he just made me feel, but I also want to somehow *tell* him, *show* him, what's happening to me inside. How he's made me feel like I matter and like I'm safe and...

I lower my mouth to him, right where a drop of moisture has beaded at the tip. I lick and suck that moisture, and I can feel him wrestling for self-control, trembling from the effort. I circle the sensitive head, tucking my tongue under the ridge, wriggling it against the part I know will be most sensitive. He curses.

My hands are on his thighs. The muscles under my touch are hard knots, and when I stroke a palm up the ridges of his abs, they clench, needy, under my fingertips. My core contracts in answer, and for a moment I think about just climbing on top of him, letting him fill me. But then he wraps a hand loosely around the back of my head and tugs on my hair, and satisfaction surges through me, refocusing me on my delicious work. I take him as deep as I can, and he groans, his hips jerking now, like he's battling with himself not to thrust.

I pop off and tell him, "It's okay. I can take more of you. I'll squeeze your thigh if I need you to stop."

He groans, his head thrown back. "Jesus, Mari. Jesus. I'll stop as soon as you need me to." And of course he will. He's Kane.

"Mari," he groans a moment later. "God, you feel so good... If you don't want me to come in your mouth—"

I grip his hip a little tighter, and with another groan and a thrust I can tell he can't hold back, he's coming hard, spasming against my tongue and my throat, calling my name.

I let him go and he collapses onto the lounge, speechless.

As I curl up next to him, he wraps his arms around me and buries his face in my hair.

Dark has fallen, and there's no light inside Bernadette right now. We sit that way for a long time.

Until he says, "I'm really glad we did this."

I burst out laughing.

"Ha—no. I mean, yes, hell, yes, I'm glad we did that. It was—so fucking good." He knocks his head back against the lounge, emphasizing the last three words. "But I meant I'm glad we did the trip together." His eyes are on mine, and even in the mostly-dark, I can see how serious his expression is, like it was earlier on the side of the road. "I needed to see it. See you on the road. It made me understand you better. I totally get it, now. How much you love the road. That you're happy here." He takes another deep breath. "The thing is, the more I get to know you and the more I care for you—"

I make a little sound of surprise, and he smiles, then, washing away the seriousness.

"Hell, yes, I care, and if I didn't think it would scare the shit out of you, I'd say more than that."

But it *doesn't* scare the shit out of me. It thrills me. And I almost say, *Tell me more. Say more. I want to hear it.*

I don't though, because he's talking again, a rush of words. "What this trip has made me realize is that I don't want to *make* you want anything. Or *convince* you of anything. The woman I care about, this country is her neighborhood. The road is her home. Every place she goes is an adventure. She's strong as steel and tougher than my brother Gabe. And—I don't want any of that to change. I don't want to change you one little bit. So if you don't want to stay in Rush Creek? Then I will find a way to be okay with that. Whatever it looks like. There are plenty of dads who spend weeks on the road every month—if that's what you need, we can figure out how to make that happen, too. We'll discuss how to talk to our kid about it, too. I know that part won't be easy, but we'll find a way to make sure this child knows it's loved."

His eyes hold mine, pale blue, endlessly sincere, and absolutely confident in what he's saying. A Wilder to the core. Nothing like his brothers, and everything like them.

"I..." I stop, mostly because I'm not sure I'll be able to squeeze the words out around the lump in my throat. But somehow, I manage.

"This trip is making me see clearly, too," I say. "I thought I was trying to find out if you'd be good for Bun."

"Bun," he repeats.

"It's what I've started calling the baby. In my head. Like your bun in my oven."

He makes a small, rusty sound. I think it's half laughter, and the other half—it's just raw emotion.

"And I don't have the slightest doubt about that. I know you'll be good for him or her or them. But the better I get to know you, the more I think you're good for *me*."

His eyes widen, then darken, the blue suddenly almost drowned by black.

"Mari," he says, his voice rough.

My chest is tight, but I know what I need to tell him.

"I can't imagine just walking away, Kane. I can't. So if it's still what you think you want, I want to give it a shot."

32

KANE

We're a couple of hours from home when I start getting frantic texts from Gabe.

Gabe: *Where are you? I need that trailer tomorrow morning crack of dawn for a trip.*

Me: *That would have been good to know before we left with it.*

Gabe: *I thought you were coming straight back! Where the hell were you?*

Me: *Seeing some sights.*

There's a long silence on the other end of the phone. Then,

Gabe: *I'm sure you were.*

Me: *What's that supposed to mean?*

More silence.

Me: *Gabe.*

Gabe: *What? Tell me you're not enjoying the scenery. I know you enjoyed it at least once in the past.*

Ah. My siblings have spread the word that the baby is mine.

I sneak a look at Mari.

Last night, after our big, serious conversation, we got into Mari's bed together and lay there, our hands on her belly, fingers intertwined across the rippling movement of our baby. We fell asleep like that, her, me, and Bun. Happiness bubbled in my chest, rich and dangerous.

The dangerous part is because I'm not foolish enough to think *I want to give it a shot* is any kind of promise.

Still, I knew how huge a step that was for her, especially after I'd told her I didn't want her to do anything she didn't feel ready to do.

And I can't rush any of this. I can only give her space and trust in what happens between us.

In the meantime, Gabe's right.

I have been enjoying the scenery.

I really enjoyed it earlier this afternoon when Mari pulled over to the side of the road and informed me that she was so on edge that the vibrations of the Airstream were driving her to distraction.

I helped her out. Of course. I'm generous like that.

I buried my hand between her legs and kissed her while I worked her until she came, fluttering and spasming against my palm and fingers, biting my lip and muffling her cries in my mouth.

"Whoops," she said, when she could talk again. She cupped a hand over the bulge in my jeans. "I pretty much just transferred the problem to you, huh?"

"Not a problem," I said, through gritted teeth, as she teased through the thick denim.

"It won't be. In a minute."

This turned out to be true, and I enjoyed *all* the scenery as she helped me out.

I jolt my brain back to the present moment and the phone in my hand.

Me: *I have no idea what you're talking about.*

Gabe: *Just get that fucking trailer back here. I don't care if you have to drive all night.*

Me: *We just met up with 395. We're only two hours out.*

Gabe: *Why didn't you just say that?*

Me: *Because I'm your brother and messing with you is more fun.*

Gabe: *You're supposed to be the brother who doesn't mess with me.*

I think about what Mari said. *That's a lot to live up to.*

I look over at her. She's humming along softly to Johnny Cash on the radio, tiny in that big driver's seat, but looking like she was born to sit there, like the queen of the whole fucking country.

Slowly, I thumb an answer. *Yeah, well, I'm supposed to be a lot of things.*

Long silence. Then:

Gabe: *The trailer, Kane. The fucking trailer. And while you're at it, a few of us are having impromptu dinner at my place. The Perezes are cooking Cuban.*

Me: *Incoming.*

"We're going to have to make a couple of stops before we go back to my place," I say. I almost said, *before we go home.* "We have to drop off the range at Clark's work site and then bring the trailer to Wilder HQ." I hesitate. "Some of my family is there having dinner. If—if you'd be interested. Rachel—"

"Brody's fiancée, right?" Lines appear between her brows. "Have they set a date?"

I shake my head. "They don't care how long it takes before they get married, and they want to do the big wedding thing, so they've been putting it off until Jessa can do it exactly the way they want it." I love so much that she's been trying to keep track of my sprawling family.

"Rachel and her family are fantastic cooks and they're making Cuban so it'll be amazing. But no pressure. I know you must be exhausted."

She holds still. I can almost see her thinking. Then she says, "I'd like that."

And it shouldn't matter so much to me, but it really fucking does.

Mari

There's some saying about how you can't dip your toe in the same stream twice. Meaning—I've always thought— that even if the riverbed stays the same, the water keeps rushing on, different molecules every second. It might look like the same river, but it isn't.

That's how I feel tonight at Gabe's house. Like I'm back here at the edge of the rushing river of Wilder energy, but it's not the same.

Well, it is—and it isn't.

I mean, the kids are still running around like a litter of puppies, making enough noise to power a small city.

The adults all still seem to have been trained since birth in how to be awesome with kids. Like Clark has organized some of the kids into a game of flag football. Only the older kids have leg weights—borrowed from Barb and her girlfriend Geneva—on their ankles so the younger kids can keep up. Who thinks of shit like that?

The Wilders, apparently.

And the kitchen is full of organized chaos. Rachel's family, the Perezes, are cooking ropa vieja, and an assortment of Wilders and Wilder significant others are helping out with side dishes. There's going to be brown rice, white rice, cauliflower rice, and black beans, and fried plantains and... Yeah. Yum.

I'm ravenous, as usual, and plan to eat it all.

Meanwhile, Buck has already stolen my shoes twice, but Lucy and Gabe are both on shoe watch, and so far the shoes have been rescued with no further trauma. Lucy did, however, grab a sweater that I left draped over a chair and insist I put it on. She said there was no other way to keep it safe from Buck. Then Gabe came up behind her and said, "You can't interfere with the natural order, Luce," and she rolled her eyes at him and told me, "Don't listen to him."

I go looking for Kane and nearly stumble into him having a quiet corner conversation with Amanda. I pull back, but it's impossible to miss Kane's words. "We're going to do this," he tells her. "We're going to raise the baby together."

His voice is buoyant, and I wait for the twinge of fear I would have felt before. The doubt. The worry that I could be the woman he needs, the mother my baby needs, someone who stays. But it doesn't come.

Amanda squeals. "I know how much you want this, Kane. I know how much you want to be a father. How much you've wanted a family. And I'm so glad you two are going to give it a shot. I think she's great. I think she's exactly what you need."

"She's amazing," he says. "But for God's sake, Amanda, please be gentle with her. She hasn't had an easy time of it."

"I will. Of course I will," she tells him. "We all will, until she doesn't need us to be."

My eyes fill with tears.

I swallow the lump in my throat, retreating into the living room with my arms wrapped around myself.

A moment later, Lucy comes in, Willow in her arms. The baby's awake, alert, and bouncing her arms and legs as she looks around. Her big blue eyes focus on me, and her mouth tips up into a smile.

She's smiling. At me.

I smile back, bring a hand up to hide my eyes, then drop my hand.

She waves her arms and legs harder and emits a baby chortle that startles me into laughter.

"She's just starting to laugh," Lucy says. "You want to hold her?"

"I—"

"Here," she says, thrusting the baby out. "There's nothing to it. She'll fuss if she doesn't like the way you hold her and calm down if you move her into a more comfortable position. Right now she's starting to like facing out."

I take the baby under her arms and pull her close to my body, so her feet, still kicking, drum against my belly. A sudden movement inside startles me. Bun, awake now, kicks back from the inside, as if she's returning a greeting.

Cousins.

Willow settles against my chest, a warm, heavy weight. Her movements still a bit, and she sighs.

"She likes you," Lucy says. "They say they know who they can trust." She smiles at me, sunshiny and gentle, and maybe this is just wishful thinking, but I feel like she's saying something else. That *she* likes me. That she *trusts* me. With her kid. Maybe even with her brother-in-law's feelings.

"Lucy," I say, "Do you think... do you think you and Amanda could maybe take me shopping for some baby stuff? I have no idea what I'm doing."

I've startled her. "I didn't realize—" she says, and then, "Of course! Absolutely. I would have said something sooner, but I wasn't sure... I wasn't sure where things stood. With you and Kane and..." She looks like she's making up her mind about something. "About whether you were staying."

"I wasn't either," I say.

I could stop there, but Lucy is watching me, expression soft and sympathetic, so I tell her the rest. How Kane and I met and got me pregnant, how I couldn't find him again, how I didn't know what I should do and how that made me slow to do anything.

"Maybe I was just *waiting*," I say.

"Maybe you were," she says. "I'm glad you did."

"Me fucking too," I say, and we both laugh.

"The trip was good," I say.

"I got that feeling," Lucy says, trying to hold back a smile, and that makes us both laugh again.

"Hey," I say. "What's the deal with Buck? What's Gabe's whole thing with him and eating people's clothes."

She hesitates.

"C'mon."

She leans close and murmurs. "He's gotten it in his head that when Buck eats something that belongs to a woman that a Wilder brother is dating, that means she's The One."

I snort laughter—but Lucy's not laughing.

My mouth drops open. "You actually believe it?"

"No. Of course not. It's total bunk," Lucy says.

"But you kind of believe it, anyway."

She looks all around, as if to make sure we're not being overheard.

"Let's just say I can't discount it yet," she whispers.

I think of my shoe, which hasn't been the same since Buck gnawed it. It should scare me, the idea of Gabe being right... but it doesn't.

Willow is getting quieter and heavier on my chest, and I turn her so her cheek rests against my shoulder. She settles there and sighs again, sinking in.

"She's going to fall asleep on you," Lucy says. "Do you mind?"

I shake my head. She smells so good, milky and clean, and when I bend my face down, I can feel the soft brush of her downy hair against my own cheek.

"Once she's asleep we can carry her upstairs and put her down."

"She can stay here as long as she wants," I say.

Lucy's gaze moves past me, soft and fond, and I think, when I turn around, that I'll see Gabe. But when I look, it's Kane, standing in the doorway, watching us, and the warmth in his eyes melts me.

33

———

KANE

After we leave Gabe's, we park Bernadette in her regular spot by my toolshed. I cut the engine, turn to look at Mari, and find her looking back at me in the dark.

I can still see her in Gabe's living room, Willow in her arms, her face tipped down to press her cheek against the baby's. I can still hear her saying, *She can stay here as long as she wants*, and those words and the way I felt, looking at her, are all mixed up with how I feel about her and what I want from her.

Right now, I just want to be as close to her as I can.

"Would you... want to sleep in the house tonight?"

There's a full moon, and her smile gleams in the dark. "Yeah. I would. Let me just grab a few things."

"Take your time," I tell her. "Bring anything you want. Stay as long as you want. Like you told Willow."

Her smile gets a little bigger. "Go on up. I'll be there in a minute."

I haul my camping stuff to the house. Unpacking takes

just a few minutes, and I'm left at loose ends, standing in my kitchen, hoping like hell she won't get cold feet.

In the meantime, I make us both mugs of hot chocolate with marshmallows. I may not be the most alpha Wilder, but I know how to woo a woman with chocolate.

Her knock comes just as I'm dropping the mini marshmallows into her mug.

I open the door to find her standing there with a small duffle, looking... shy. There's a little twist to her shoulders, like a kid who isn't completely sure of herself. And I think, honestly, it's the first time I've seen that, seen her look like she doesn't know what she wants or what she's doing.

Between seeing her with Willow on her chest, hearing her say Willow could stay there as long as she needed to, and the way she looks right now—I'm wrecked. But then, I never really stood a chance.

"Hot cocoa on the kitchen counter," I say.

I didn't clear a drawer in the bathroom or my dresser. I didn't empty hangers. I'm not going to make a big thing about the duffel bag or a house key. Because even though I know we're walking towards something big together, I also meant what I said to her about not caging her.

She has to come to it—if she does—and stay—if she can—on her own terms.

She drops her duffel on the kitchen floor with a whoop and picks up her cocoa mug. "I love hot chocolate with marshmallows," she says.

"And this is really good cocoa."

She tastes it. "Oh, man, that *is*."

"Made locally," I say, eyebrows up. "Lotta good things in Rush Creek."

She grins. "I'm getting that." She licks her lips but misses a small swath of cocoa mustache.

I wipe away the mustache with my finger, lingering on her lower lip. Then I lick the remaining drop off my finger. Her eyes get that dazed look. She sets her cocoa down.

"You know what's really good in Rush Creek?" she asks.

"Mmm?"

"The *sex*." She comes close and kisses me, chocolate and warm and deliciously her. Her mouth is already open, her arms twining around me, and I tug her close. We pause to laugh at her belly between us. "So frustrating," she says, and I can hear it in her voice.

"I love your pregnancy hormones," I tell her.

"It might be that or it might be you," she says. "It was like this in Vegas, too."

"I know," I groan, and then I groan again because she's taken my hand and pulled it between her legs, where she's hot and swollen and a little damp through her leggings.

"Please make me come like you did on the road," she says. "I'm so close already."

I groan, my cock surging. "I have a better idea."

I scoop her up and carry her to my bedroom, gently deposit her on the bed.

"I like this idea," she tells me. Her eyes are hazy with lust, her lower lip soft. I bend to kiss her, and she moans and tries to pull me down. But I am on a mission now. I slide her shoes and socks off, tug her leggings down. Then her panties. I need her help to get her shirt off, and she's uncoordinated now, so we struggle a little, laughing.

I stop laughing, though, when I see her.

"God," I say. "Look at you."

I show her, tracing over the taut skin of breasts and belly, lingering on her big, sensitive nipples, until she's panting.

"Kane. Please. Hurry."

I tug my own clothes off while she watches. I'm ridiculously hard, my cock bouncing off my own stomach when I free it.

"I want to look at you too," she says. "You're beautiful." She rises to her knees and strokes a hand over my stomach, up my chest. Both palms on my pecs, her eyes closed like she's memorizing the feel of me. I bend and kiss her, and she whimpers.

"You said hurry."

"I know, but I haven't gotten to look *and* touch before, and—" She licks my nipple, then makes her way down, down, downward, licking once, maddeningly, tantalizingly, around the head of my cock. She pulls back and surveys me again. "Even your cock is beautiful."

"I'll take the compliment, but... penises aren't beautiful."

"No, they are, they really are, and I would really like this one inside me. Like, now."

"Uh. Yeah. I can do that. Do you want me to wear a condom?" I ask. "I'm clean. I had a checkup a week before you arrived, and no sex since then."

She shakes her head. "I'm clean too."

"How—what's best for you?"

"Maybe me on top?"

"Not fighting you on that."

I lie down and she throws a leg over me so her wet heat meets my erection. My hips jerk up. I want to bury myself in her so bad, it's almost painful. But she's teasing now, working herself along my length, tipping toward me to get contact on her clit, her eyes going distant each time she gets what she needs. I reach up and cup her breasts, one in each hand, thumbs playing over her nipples, and she says, "Oh, *God*, Kane, you're going to make me come so fast. It's going to be ridiculous." She's rocking herself back and forth on me, and she's already pretty far gone, a mottled red flush on her chest and throat, her eyes unfocused.

"Let me in," I tell her, and she does, sliding back, working a hand between us, and guiding me into her.

"God, Mari, that's—"

"Kane!"

She rises and falls on me, and she's tight and wet and it feels so fucking good I almost just let go. But I don't. Because she's still rocking, seeking, her breasts pressed into my hands, eyes finding some far-off spot, and I want to get her there more than I want it for myself. I sit up enough to take a nipple into my mouth, and she cries out and goes over, contracting hard around me, milking me, head thrown back, my name on her lips.

And then I'm gone, too, following her, pouring myself into her wet heat and telling her how fucking sexy she is, how much I love being inside her, how much I want to do this again and again and again.

"You're staring," she says.

"I'm sorry." I think about it a moment. "Mmm. Not sorry."

"Don't be. I like it."

"Good. Because I don't think I can stop."

We're lying on our sides, facing each other. I don't know about her, but I don't feel like I can move any time soon. In fact, my limbs don't really feel like they belong to me.

They don't, really. They belong to her, along with my heart and the whole rest of me.

And I don't want to stop staring at her because she's all lush curves and outrageous swoops and whorls, like those rocks in Black Magic Canyon. The big globe of her belly, bisected from the navel down with a darker line, the spectacular swells of her breasts, with their big areolae and nipples a little abraded from being lavished with my slightly scruffy affections. The bright triangle of curls between her legs where her soft, lightly freckled thighs are pressed together.

I want my camera.

She notices. "What are you thinking?"

"I'm not sure I should say it out loud."

"You know you should."

"I want photos. I want to take pictures. Right now. Of you like this."

Her lips curve, too. "You could do that."

"Are you sure?"

"I'm sure."

"I would never show them to anyone."

"Don't promise that," she says. "You're going to be famous one day, and I want to see my pregnant self in a gallery."

"You do not. Not really."

"I do. Really and truly. I'm not self-conscious. And

besides, I trust you to make me look beautiful. You make everything you see beautiful."

It probably wouldn't have mattered what she said after *I trust you,* but the rest of the sentence pretty much destroys me.

I roll out of bed, naked. She watches me walk across the room, and when I look back, she's biting her lip. My cock, which moments ago was all about the rest-and-relaxation, gets heavy again.

I collect my camera.

"How do you want me?"

"In every position on every surface of my house, several times a day, for the rest of our lives," I say, before I can stop myself.

She just smiles.

"Oh, you mean the pose."

She laughs.

I think about it for a minute. It's not just her body I want to capture. It's her whole energy, the way it feels to be in a room with her.

No. The way it feels to be on the road with her.

And then I know.

"In Bernadette," I tell her.

"Wait, what?" I say, when Lucy puts the Bag Balm—lotion for my nipples—into the cart.

"Trust me," she says.

I raise my eyebrows. "You want me to buy something that's made for cow udders, and you think I should trust you?"

"Not to put too fine a point on it," Amanda says. "But you are about to have the human equivalent of udders."

I whimper.

It took us almost three weeks to find a date when the three of us could go shopping together for baby things, but here we are. And none too soon, either, because I'm officially in my last month. Huge, and counting down. At this point—Lucy's OB reassures me—even if the baby came early, he or she would likely be ready for the world.

For the past three weeks, I've been staying in Kane's house.

We've had a lot more sex. We've experimented with different positions. They're all amazing, basically. Sex with Kane is in a class of its own, which is a thing I've known since Vegas. I try to work out all the reasons. He's big and he knows how to use his size, which not all big guys do. He's careful and generous and solicitous. He always, always makes me come first, even when I can tell it's practically killing him, like that first time in his bed.

But I still think it's more about how I feel when I'm with Kane, which is absolutely, completely, and totally *safe*.

And not at all in the boring way, because there is *nothing* boring about what we've been doing these last few weeks, since we got back from our trip.

In the meantime, I've been working my ass off on the plans for the trailers. Clark and I have found a bunch of contractors who can do the dirty work I can't right now—under my supervision—and locate the remaining supplies we need. For a few days, I thought Kane and I might have to hit the road again to find them, but we've been able to get everyone to ship us what we need for a reasonable price.

When neither of us is working, he feeds me breakfast, bakes me Boston cream pies, massages my feet, makes me cocoa, and gives me orgasm after orgasm.

I look inside myself daily for signs that I need to reconsider my decision, but there are none. I don't feel itchy or antsy or eager to hit the road. I just feel...

Happy.

I'm happy.

Maybe the happiest I've been my whole life.

Part of me wants to call my mother and tell her. *You were wrong! I was wrong! I'm not like you.*

But the other part of me doesn't want to know what she'd say in return.

Lucy deposits a twelve-pack of swaddle blankets into the cart.

"Are you sure we need that many?" I'm keeping a running tally of the costs in my head, and even though Kane told me not to stress about it, it's... a lot.

"Yes," Amanda says. "Because you might get lucky and have a kid who doesn't spit up, but if you do, it's because your genes overrode the Wilder baby barf genes."

I close my eyes.

"You're going to be fine," Lucy says comfortingly. "We are going to make sure of it."

Amanda adds several multi-packs of bottles and nipples to the cart. She's been racing back and forth as we shop, bringing things and putting them in my cart, explaining why they're essential and how I'll use them. She's also been giving me terrifying amounts of labor advice—and she practically ordered Kane and me to take a hypnobirthing class, which she says was life changing. Hypnobirthing, it turns out, is a way of training your brain so when it hears a certain word, it sends a deep relaxation message to your body. And who can't use a little more relaxation? So Kane and I have been going.

"Why do I need so many bottles?"

Lucy puts a hand on my arm. "I leave a bottle, a couple diapers, a complete change of clothes, and a blanket at every Wilder house, because invariably, I forget something in the diaper bag, and I'm beyond grateful to have them."

"And they don't mind?"

"Are you kidding? They fight to have Willow and me

come visit. If leaving supplies at their houses makes us visit, they're all in. It's going to be the same way with Bun."

I've told Amanda and Lucy that Kane and I call my baby Bun. They think it's adorable.

My baby.

I'm letting myself think it now, and it's not even terrifying.

The shopping trip goes on that way, with me asking why and them regaling me with scarier and scarier explanations.

And yet, my overriding feeling is of excitement. The more baby equipment they introduce me to, to more I can't wait to meet my actual baby.

We finish up and are standing in line at the register when Lucy and Amanda simultaneously reach for their cell phones.

"Uh-oh," Lucy says.

"Everyone OK?"

Amanda, too, is scanning her texts.

"Oh my God, you have to be *kidding* me," she says.

"What?"

"We have to go rescue Hanna."

"From—?"

"She's on a date. With *Nan's nephew*."

"Nan—like bakery Nan?"

"Mmm-hmm. He took her geocaching and his car broke down at the entrance to the forest." She holds up her phone.

Hanna: HELP!

Hanna: The tow truck is 90 minutes out.

Hanna: Someone is feeding him lines. Like, he's a stammering mess and then every once in a while he'll look down at his phone and then look up at me and say, "Hanna. You're wonderful to be so patient with me about this." He's literally reading off the screen.

Hanna: OMG. I just caught a glimpse of the thread. It's NAN! NAN is feeding him romantic lines!

Lucy claps her hand to her face. "Nan is Cyrano-ing her nephew!"

Amanda looks faintly green. "That's—I can't even..."

Hanna: Please come get me.

THIRTY-THREE MINUTES LATER, Hanna is in the back seat of Lucy's car, she and Amanda flanking Willow, who is sacked out sleeping.

"I'm so sorry, Hanna," Lucy says. "That must have been extremely traumatic."

"It was bad," Hanna says. "He told me he liked his women 'sturdily built' and said some guys like waifs but he appreciates someone with 'good, child-bearing hips.'"

"Noooo," Amanda says. "Please tell me Nan didn't feed him that line."

"I can't promise that," Hanna says darkly. "Also, I fucking hate geocaching. It makes me feel like an eight-year-old kid on a treasure hunt. And who goes on a hike without bringing snacks? Luckily, I had a power bar and a water bottle, but this was a *date!* Whatever happened to picnics?"

She sighs heavily. "The thing is? This wasn't even the worst date I've been on."

"Okay if I bring Mari into the loop?" Amanda asks. "We know more backstory than she does."

"Oh, yeah, sorry, Mari. I had this dumbass idea that maybe I'd try to, I don't know, at least get *laid*. And maybe meet someone I actually liked. Not like a whole long-term relationship with marriage and kids. And someone shoot me if I ever put on a white dress and walk down an aisle in a church. But—"

She stops. "It can get lonely sometimes."

I don't know Hanna well, but I don't get the impression she says stuff like that very often. "It can," I say, matter-of-factly. I have the feeling that if I say too much or get too chummy, I'll scare her off—but I've so been there.

"Anyway," Hanna says, waving off my sympathy. I don't take it personally. "I've been trying stuff. Online dating. Tinder. I've even gone to a couple of singles events." She closes her eyes in an expression that I read as *The horror!*

She opens her eyes. "All disasters. There are two basic categories of candidates. Out of towners and locals. Out of towners are either—" She holds up a hand to tick the possibilities off on her fingers—"married, or not interested in anything except one night, by which they mean one night of getting their rocks off and then falling sound asleep while I sneak out so I can go home and finish myself in peace."

Amanda makes an outraged sound. "Are you *serious*?"

"Dead serious."

"That's—"

"More common than you'd think." Hanna rakes a hand

through her short hair. "And then there are the locals. Much less likely to be married, because they know they'll get caught. I have to assume they'd also be more generous in bed, simply because they know I'm gonna tell my girl-friends if they're selfish assholes in the sack. But I wouldn't know, because I haven't actually met a local I like enough to get in bed with. The last two? The undertaker for Ford-with's Funeral Home—who was nice, but, like twenty years older than me and seriously, seriously smelled like flowers. And I *like* flowers, but I just couldn't stop thinking about the flowers and the caskets and the bodies. Poor dude. But no. And. Cone of silence?"

"Cone of silence," Amanda says, drawing a cone around her head. Lucy mimics the gesture one-handed. I've never heard of cone of silence, but I do it too. Not sure who I'd tell, because all my friends are in this car, but it feels worth the promise.

"Did you know Mack Gault was a *porn star*?"

"Who's Mack Gault?"

"A very hot ex-rodeo star," Amanda explains. "I'm not surprised, for reasons I can't elaborate on."

"Right? I mean, you don't have to elaborate. Unless he's bluffing, the reasons are, erm, front and center. Anyway, he asked me out, and I was, like, YES! Like in the sense of Sally in the deli in *When Harry Met Sally*. Except—and seriously, you cannot tell *anyone*—he wanted me to sign a release before we had sex. Because he wanted to *film us*. Because he wants to use the footage to try to get his career back on track! Which is noble, but *no! No, no, no!*"

"Noble and *flattering*," I say thoughtfully.

"It is flattering!" Hanna preens a bit.

"And maybe... almost worth it?"

Hanna laughs. "The thought crossed my mind. But you could never, ever get that back if it went up on the Internet."

"True, true," I say.

We all think about it for a bit.

"I mean, there are certain droughts in my life where I would have done it," I admit.

"Yeah," Lucy says. "Me too."

"Not me," Amanda says.

"Easy for you," Hanna says carelessly. "You've been having earth-shattering sex with Heath since you were, what, like, nineteen? You don't have droughts."

"I so *did!* And you know it."

"Yeah, but then your hero Heath fixed it all and then some with his magic wang." Hanna heaves her biggest sigh yet. "I'm starting to think there's a reason I didn't date for five years," she says.

"Have you been dating women, too?" Amanda asks her.

Hanna shrugs. "A few. One was super cute but, again, *married!* What the heck, people? Doesn't anyone respect vows anymore? And the other two the chemistry just wasn't there." Hanna turns to me. "I'm bi," she says, with another of her shrugs.

"I figured that out from context," I say, grinning.

"Anyway," Hanna says, with another lift of a shoulder, "I think I might be ready to give up on dating."

"Don't give up!" Amanda says. "Your prince charming could be right around the corner."

"Let's hope not," Hanna says. "If he is, he probably makes golden shower porn for a living and is going to make me sign a release before I use the toilet so he can film me and resuscitate his career."

We all wince.

"That *definitely* wouldn't be worth the hassle of going viral," I mutter.

I'm rewarded with a burst of their laughter.

35

KANE

"Hey," I say to a barista I recognize slightly. I think she's a high school classmate of Amanda's. "Is Kelsey in?" Kelsey owns Morning Rush coffee, which is where I am right now, breathing in the rich scents of coffee roasted on the premises, and bacon, egg, and cheese sandwiches.

The walls of the coffee shop are decked with bright-colored art. Even in its rodeo days, Rush Creek had its share of artists attracted by the solitude of the mountains and the beautiful scenery, and that community has only grown more vibrant in the last couple of years, drawn by the hot springs.

"She's in the back. Who do you want me to say is here?"

"Kane Wilder," I say. "I'm here to ask about exhibiting some photos."

I ordered a bunch of 16 x 20 prints of my favorite photos from the lab I like working with, and I've got them in a portfolio I'm carrying at my side. My heart's in my throat. I honestly think a rejection from Kelsey might feel worse than that breakup by Veronica's parents, which now seems hilarious, fated, and ancient. I can't believe I thought Veronica was right for me. For that matter, I can't believe I thought any of the women I've dated in the last decade was the one, as if all I needed was a girl with a Rush Creek address and glossy hair to be happy.

Turns out I was looking for something completely different.

The barista comes back. "She'll be out in a few. In the meantime, have a seat, and she says coffee's on us. What can I get you?"

"Dark roast would be great."

She bustles behind the counter and hands me a to-go cup. I grab a table in the back corner and check my phone for texts. I've gotten in the habit of checking in frequently, because Mari could go into labor at any point.

She doesn't know I'm here at the coffee shop, showing my photos. I guess part of me wanted it to be a surprise for her if it worked out. And if it didn't—well, I guess I wasn't sure I wanted her to know that.

She and the Wilder Woman Squad—as I secretly think of them—are back at my house, painting the nursery, previously known as the guest bedroom. Well, the others are painting; Mari's supervising from just out of paint-fumes range. I offered to help and was flat-out rejected—by *my own sister*. Which if I'm being truthful made me super happy. I love that Mari is bonding with the other women.

Mari came back elated from her baby-gear shopping day a week ago.

I'd wanted to go on that outing, but some instinct told me not to invite myself along, and I'm glad I didn't. Something happened on that trip that brought Mari into the fold. Since then, Mari's been out with one of her women friends as often as she's been home with me.

Which—I will say it again—I regard as evidence of victory. I always knew I wasn't going to win her over on the strength of my own personality. It takes a village to make a new Wilder.

Kelsey comes out from the Morning Rush kitchen, wiping her hands on her apron, leaving dark black streaks. When my eyes catch on the sight, her gaze follows mine, and she sighs. "Espresso machine broke. Fixing it's a bitch and an unholy mess. You have something to show me?"

She hews to a particular Pacific Northwest type: gray hair, super fit, head-to-toe athletic wear including running shoes.

We move to a table where I open my portfolio. Then I lunge and manage to just catch my coffee before I knock it everywhere.

"That would have been unfortunate," Kelsey says.

"At least they're photographs and not pastels."

"Ha," she says. "So true." She sits down and pages through my work. I try not to look over her shoulder, but I can't help myself. I try to see my work through her eyes and read her expression for her reactions. The photo of Amanda and Anna is in there. The one of Mari in the Sluice Box, and then the series of photos of her, naked and almost nine full months pregnant, moving around the inside of her Airstream.

Kelsey's got a good poker face, though, and watching her only knots up my stomach, so I tell her I'm going to take a quick walk and step outside the coffee shop, where I pace the sidewalk, wishing I could bundle my photos up and take them away from her prying eyes.

This was a bad idea. Lots of people take photos. Lots of people take good photos, even. It doesn't mean they're good enough to be on display.

She waves through the window for me to come back inside. She's closed the portfolio, and she's still expression-less. I brace myself for rejection.

"How long have you been taking photos?" she asks.

"My whole life," I say.

"But you've never exhibited them. Not once?"

I shake my head.

She gives me a thoughtful look.

"I would love to exhibit these," she says, smiling. Finally. "They're amazing. But there's someone else I think needs to see them first."

36

———

MARI

The FaceTime call wakes me at 7 am. I grab the phone before Kane can be roused, haul my whale-self out of bed, and waddle into the kitchen. My back aches. It's been bothering me a lot the last couple of days, but I must have slept funny, because today it's fierce. I press my hand to the achy spot, and the pain subsides.

"Hey, Mom." I keep my voice low.

Every time I say it, I wonder if I should just call her Lori. And yet there's still this small part of me, the part of me that remembers the adventures and the good times, that can't give up the childhood name: Mom.

"Hi, Mari!" she says. She's in an up mood today, which is good. Our calls go better when she is.

I lean the phone against Kane's flour canister while I start a pot of coffee. Not for me, for Kane. It's a habit we've gotten into lately. I wake up earlier, usually, because the baby is kicking my bladder. So I brew coffee for Kane, who wakes up, drinks the coffee, and cooks breakfast for me.

My back pain flares again, and I rub a hand over the sore part. I'll ask Kane for a back massage when he wakes up.

"Where are you?" my mom asks. That's always one of the first questions we ask each other.

"Still in Rush Creek," I tell her. I'd sent her a couple of texts right after I landed here to let her know that I was doing a job and would be staying put for a bit.

"Still?" she says. "Huh. I have to be in Portland next week. I could stop by and see you."

Something freezes in my chest. "Sure, Mom." I swallow hard.

"I know I didn't show the last time, but that was different."

"Yeah?" I ask, trying to keep my voice even. She's talking about the last time she said she'd "stop by," when I was doing a job in Iowa City and she was crossing the country on her way to Philadelphia.

It never happened. A few days after she'd said she'd arrive, she called me from the East coast to say she hadn't had time to stop, after all.

"Yeah. I had a deadline that time, and I was running behind. This time I don't have anywhere to be."

"Uh-huh," I say, one hand idly massaging my back.

I hear the sounds of Kane rustling out of bed in the room behind me, and my heart turns over. I should have known better than to take the call in the house, when he could walk in. It's not rational, I know it's not, but I don't want to have to explain Kane, or what I'm doing with him, to my mother.

"Morning, sunshine!" he calls, and his bare-torso-self

steps into the kitchen. He is golden and better than breakfast.

"Whoa," my mother says. She leans towards the camera, like that might let her peer around me. She can't, of course. "Who's that?"

"Mom, this is Kane. Kane, this is my mom. Lori."

"Hi, Lori," Kane says, waving.

"Hi, Kane." My mom gives me great big WTF eyes.

"Coffee's ready," I say, then snatch up the phone and take it into the bedroom.

"Mari." My mom's definitely curious. "Who is that hottie?"

"I told you. That's Kane."

Something in my voice must tip her off. She frowns at me. "Are you *living* with him?" And then, even more fiercely. "Mari, he's not—he's not the dad, is he?"

As much as I don't want to answer, Kane matters to me, and I don't want to make him into a lie. Not even to avoid a showdown with my mother. "Yeah. He's the dad."

"I thought you didn't know who the dad was."

In a few brushstrokes, I catch her up on the story. How I met both Clark and Kane in Vegas separately and didn't realize they were brothers, how Kane and I hooked up, and eventually Clark summoned me to do the work we'd talked about in Vegas.

"So, what, you're all bunked up like a happy family?" she demands. "What happened to looking for an adoption?"

I think of the self I was a few weeks ago, lying in bed with my phone out and the adoption profiles up. Still believing what I'd told myself, that I was too much like my mother to do this right.

"I changed my mind," I say. "Things changed, and I changed my mind."

She draws a sharp breath. "Mari, that's not a good idea. Take it from me, sweetheart. It'll be fun for a little bit, and then you'll go out of your ever-loving mind. You'll last a year, and then what? Are you going to take the baby with you on the road? Or leave it with some guy you don't even know? It's not too late to change your mind again. Seriously, hon, listen: You know how the Barrymores are. We're wanderers."

These are the words she said to me when she gave me the bracelet. She's repeated those words to me tens of times since.

Those words, they've always felt like a mallet striking a gong with the ring of truth.

But something's different this time.

Maybe it was her saying, "Some guy you don't even know." Because it doesn't feel like that describes Kane at all. Kane's not some guy. He's—

He's *my guy*.

He's not just hot breakfast and homemade Boston cream pie and foot massages. He's adventure and safety, zing and physical comfort.

He's thoughtful and generous and creative and loving.

And he makes me want to stay put.

"Thanks for the warning, Mom," I say. "I know you're worried about me, but I'm going to be fine."

"That's what you think *now*," she says. "But just you wait, Mari. Wait till the baby won't stop crying and you're nursing around the clock and you know you're going to have to live the rest of your life in the same small town with the same small-minded people. You think you care about this guy, but it's not going to be enough then—"

Bun gives a gigantic kick of outrage, straight into my bladder. There's a *ping* sensation, and fluid trickles down my leg.

For a split second, I think what any non-pregnant human would think in this situation: Holy crap, I wet myself!

And then I remember something Lucy said when we were shopping for baby clothes: *When your amniotic sac breaks, you're going to think you wet yourself.*

"Mom," I say firmly. "I have to go."

I end the call and turn to find Kane behind me. His mouth is open as if he's about to say something. But before he can get the words out, a hard, mean cramp wraps around from my back to my belly, and a sharp sound of alarm jumps out of me.

"Mari!" Kane leaps to my side.

Oh. That wasn't back pain earlier.

That was...

Labor.

37

KANE

My daughter is a sweet, sleepy weight in my arms. She's snoozing, her eyes squeezed shut, her tiny fists tightly clenched, her itty-bitty heart-shaped mouth red and perfect.

She is perfect.

"You were *brilliant*," I tell Mari.

And I mean it. Hell yes, I do.

Any thoughts I had that Mari was a pixie or a waif or any of those things?

Crushed to a pulp, along with my hand, which she held and squeezed and punished through fifteen hours of labor, as she doggedly and mostly without complaint pushed an almost-eight-pound-baby into the world.

The only complaining was when she yelled at me, midway through the brutal period of time that the nurse insisted on calling "transition," that she was never having sex with me or anyone else ever again because *no sex was good enough to justify this bullshit.*

She claims not to remember saying that.

"Let me see her again," Mari says, and for the thousandth time I bend down and show her.

Mari puts out her hand and strokes our baby's soft, silky cheek. Tears drip down her face. Her face is pale and pixelated with red dots—broken blood vessels from pushing—and she has never looked more beautiful to me.

"We can't keep calling her 'Bun,'" Mari says.

"Probably not," I agree.

"What was your dad's name?"

Something clenches in my chest, a fierce, unsettling mix of joy and grief. "Zach," I say, smiling despite myself. "I don't think she'll appreciate that."

"What about... Zara?"

I close my eyes against my own tears. "I like that."

Just then, a commotion in the hallway materializes into a seething clump of Wilder family and friends. They spill into the room—Amanda, Lucy, Jessa, Hanna, Gabe, Clark, and my mother, all talking at once. I look down at Mari, who is so exhausted that she's been nodding off in the middle of our conversations for the last hour or so. I expect her to look overwhelmed, and I prepare myself to give a speech kicking everyone out so we can rest, but the expression on Mari's face is soft and warm, cracked open with gratitude and appreciation. She holds out her hands, and Lucy and Amanda each take one. They bend over the bed, whispering to her, and I can't hear much, but I know they're words of support and love and congratulations.

Gabe hands me a chocolate cigar and Clark claps me on the back, and then they just flank me, silent, as if they're saying, *We're here*, which is shockingly comforting. But at the same time, I'm not surprised by the show of support, because my brothers are the best of men.

I love my family so fucking much.

I realize something in that moment. Forever more, *my family* will mean something different than it has ever meant before. Zara has made the three of us into a family.

She has made Mari part of the Wilder family.

She has changed everything, in the best possible way.

I swipe a hand across my eyes, and when Gabe catches me doing it, he smiles and nods, a softness on his face that's so unlike him that it almost makes me cry for real.

"May I?" my mother asks. There are tears on her face, too, as she takes Zara.

"We're calling her Zara. After dad," I tell her.

Now she's openly weeping; I wipe a tear off Zara's face and then hers.

"Hello, baby," my mother says, kissing Zara all over her little face. Kissing each clenched fist and the top of her head.

Hanna leans over the bundle that is my daughter. "She's really *red*."

Amanda snorts. "They *all* look like that," she says. "Well, except Kieran, who had bright blue hands and feet, and Noah, who turned orange on day three. Red is much better, take my word for it."

"I think she's absolutely perfect," Lucy says loyally, giving Mari a high five.

Our visitors pass Zara around, taking turns oohing and ahhing and cooing over her, and fussing over Mari. Lucy and Amanda make her tell *the whole story, don't leave anything out!*

She leaves out the part where she swears off sex forever. Fingers crossed that's a good sign for me.

I don't even have to shoo everyone out, because after about fifteen minutes, Amanda claps her hands. "All right, peeps, let's leave these guys alone. Speaking from experience, Mari needs every minute of sleep she can get." She herds them out of the room, leaving us in the sudden quiet.

Zara is back in my arms. I look over at Mari.

Amanda's words couldn't have been truer: She's already sound asleep.

38

———————

MARI

For the first three days, everything is okay. Better than okay.

There are hard parts, of course. I have to figure out nursing, and it doesn't come naturally to either Zara or me. A lactation consultant comes in, and after an hour of arranging and rearranging Zara's little face against my big swollen boob, we finally achieve a "latch" that she approves of. When Zara nurses, I study the curve of her face with wonder, seeing hints of Kane, Amanda, and Barb in her features.

Kane has to teach me to change diapers, and the nurse has to teach both of us to give a bath. She seems shocked to discover that this isn't a skill we were born with. But we're fast learners and Kane is next to me every step of the way— well, except for not having boobs. He can't help that part. But he does all the changing and burping and hands me Zara, clean and sweet, to feed.

When we take her home from the hospital, she cries in the car seat, and exhausted, I weep a little, too, not sure if she's okay or hurting, or if she'll ever be able to ride in the car without crying.

By the third day my boobs are as hard as rocks, but we spend the first night in Kane's house together, the two of us in bed and Zara swaddled in a bassinet beside us, and even though I can't really let Kane cuddle me because my boobs hurt too much—and so does everything from my waist down—it still feels pretty wonderful.

Then comes the fourth day.

ON THE FOURTH DAY, for reasons known only to Zara and God, she wakes up and wants to nurse loads more.

Kane keeps burping and changing her and trying to rock her to sleep, but she fusses and cries and he has to bring her back to me again.

My nipples are sore and I'm exhausted, because last night wasn't great, either.

We run out of wipes. We both thought there were more packs somewhere, but we can't find them anywhere. Kane has to go to the grocery store to get them. While he's gone, I nurse Zara until she's in a milk coma, and she conks out against my breast. I breathe a deep sigh of relief and drift into sleep myself, baby in arms. But I'm wakened by my phone vibrating next to me.

My mom.

I remember that she's supposed to be in Portland this week, and that she said she'd stop by. For the first time in years, I feel a sharp longing for her, if only so I can ask her if it was like this for her, too. How long it lasted, how she lived through it.

My mother could be comforting when it fit her plans. I remember her holding my hair back when I was sick, cuddling me in bed.

I grab it and swipe it open. Yes, I'm half naked. No, I don't care.

"Goldy girl!" she says, beaming at me, and I remember, with a surge of something that might be love, that once upon a time, she was the center of my universe, like I'm Zara's now.

"Hi, mom. I had a baby."

"So you did," she says. "Can you turn her so I can see her face?"

"I'm afraid to move her. This is the first time she's been calm in hours."

"Another time then," she says, with a small shrug. "You're keeping her, huh?"

I ignore that—too tired to take it on—and instead ask, "Are you in the area?"

"What?" Her face is blank, like the question's absurd. "Oh. No. I decided to skip Portland after all."

I'm not surprised. I shouldn't be surprised. And yet somehow it catches me like a punch to the gut.

Maybe Zara feels it, the bloom of pain in my chest, the rush of adrenaline through my veins, because she wakes up right then and starts to fuss.

"That noise!" my mother says. "It goes straight through your brain like a nail through cheese. I'm hanging up now. Call me when she's calm sometime."

She ends the call.

Zara chooses that moment to escalate to her fussing to wailing.

Kane

Mari nurses and nurses but Zara won't stop fussing. Mari's nipples are red and chafed. I bring her scrambled eggs with bacon and a tumbler of water. I change and bathe and rock Zara, and I coax a little sleep out of her, but then she's up again, mouth open, fussing.

Mari dutifully nurses again, but after a while, tears start streaming down Mari's face, and then she's crying, her shoulders heaving.

"Don't cry, you're doing great," I say, but that makes her cry more.

Wait till the baby won't stop crying and you're nursing around the clock...

Mari's mom's words echo through my brain. Mari and I never got a chance to talk about that phone call, because she went into labor right then, and everything since has been a blur.

Mari sounded strong that day, on the phone with her mom. Strong and certain. *Thanks for the warning, Mom,* she'd said. *I know you're worried about me, but I'm going to be fine.*

She doesn't seem fine right now, however. She seems anything but fine.

"Mari?" I ask. "Unless you tell me flat out you don't want me to? I'm calling my mom and my sister."

She closes her eyes. I take it as a yes.

I grab my phone and send an SOS text.

I need reinforcements.

Mari

"Shhh," someone says. "You're going to be all right."

The same someone takes Zara from me. Lucy. She lays her down on a blanket on the floor, swaddles her with a few expert twists, and scoops her up again. A moment later she sweeps her out of the room, trailing a loud "shushing" sound behind her.

"What's she doing?"

"Don't worry about that," someone else says. Amanda. "Drink this."

I take the cup of hot tea and obediently sip it.

"It has fennel and fenugreek in it. It'll help with your milk."

Amanda sits on one side of me, Barb on the other. They each put a hand on my arm. Just that. No words.

After a moment or two, Amanda takes my tea and hands me my abandoned nursing bra, and I realize I'm naked from the waist up. My boyfriend's sister and his mother are here and I'm not wearing clothes.

And I didn't even notice.

I slip into the bra and sip the tea. I can hear Zara fussing intermittently in the other room. Every time she does, my milk lets down.

The fussing subsides more and more, and then there's only the sound of shushing. But my tears won't stop falling. I'm so tired.

And I'm so *bad* at this.

Even Kane is better at it than I am. At least he knew how to change a diaper. And he's more confident with the baths. And he doesn't fall apart into a whimpering mess every time she cries.

"Where's Kane?" I finally ask. I'm not sure how much time has passed since they arrived.

"I sent him on an errand. Lucy rented a hospital grade pump for you. We'll show you how to use it. So you can start pumping once or twice a day and Kane can give her some bottles. You have no idea how much that'll help. I sent Kane to pick it up."

"That's—thank you."

The idea of not having to feed her absolutely every time she cries? Makes *me* feel like weeping again, with relief.

Lucy comes back into view, Zara slumped against her shoulder.

"Asleep?" I ask.

"Asleep," she affirms.

I burst into tears all over again. "I couldn't calm her down."

"It's because you're the milk," Amanda says. "Sometimes someone else has to do it."

"I couldn't make her happy."

"Shhh," Lucy says. "You're okay. You need to drink the tea and then you need to nap while we hold Zara."

"I can't," I wail. "I can't nap. She'll wake up and need to be fed and I'm the only one—"

"You can nap. She'll be fine for a little while. I think she finally got enough," Lucy says.

I cry harder.

"You're all right, hon," Lucy says. "This is the hardest day. She's on a growth spurt and trying to gain back to her birth weight and all the hormones go bonkers on day four. It feels impossible. You just have to trust me; it gets easier again."

"But what if it doesn't?" I sob. "I can't do this. I can't. I can't, I can't, I can't, I can't do this, I can't do this, you're going to have to tell him I can't do this—"

A sound makes me look up. Kane is standing in the doorway, a small satchel over his shoulder. His eyes are big and shocked.

"Kane," Amanda says. "Wait."

But he doesn't. He hands the satchel to his sister, turns on a heel, and goes out the door.

Amanda and Lucy exchange looks.

"I got her," Lucy says.

"I got him," Amanda says.

And, getting to her feet, she chases Kane out the door.

39

———————

KANE

"Don't be an idiot!"

I'm halfway into the driver's seat of the Subaru when Amanda catches up to me and grabs my arm.

"She doesn't mean it!"

I try to wrestle my arm out of her grasp, but Amanda grew up fighting Wilders, and she's strong. I only succeed in tiring both of us out and pissing her off.

"Just hold still and listen!" she cries, exasperated. "This is exactly how it always happens. I swear to you, Kane. Just *listen*."

Holding still turns out to be much worse than running, because when I do what she's asked—hold still and listen—I can hear Mari's sobs in my head.

I can't do this, I can't do this.

You're going to have to tell him I can't do this...

"When Anna was four days old," Amanda starts, but the pressure in my chest is too much.

"I mean, why *would* she stay? She told me she loved her

life on the road. She told me from the very beginning. What was I thinking, trying to keep her here? I'm not the guy who makes a woman change her life. I'm not the guy with the big grand gesture. I'm not a warrior or a leader of men or a charmer—"

I stop.

Amanda watches me quietly. "No," she says. "You're not Clark or Gabe or Easton or Brody."

Startled, I make a sound of protest, but she holds up a hand.

"You're *Kane*. You listen. You pay attention. You *see* what's going on for the people you love. You help them get what they need. And you *love* her."

She's knocked the breath out of me. The way she says it. Fierce. Like me being Kane and my loving Mari are *enough*.

Like they might be all it takes to hold onto Mari forever.

Like she doesn't doubt it, at all.

Like being the boy next door isn't something to run away from, but something to be proud of.

"How do you know I love her? I haven't even told her—"

She shakes her head and rolls her eyes. "Come on, Kane, this is me. I knew that night at Gabe's when I was babbling about the baby being yours and you snapped at me. I've never seen you snap at anyone before that. I didn't even know you could." She grins. "But you were paying attention right? You knew what she needed, and you fought for her. That's what I'm talking about. That's why she would stay. Now, are you ready to fucking listen to me?" she demands.

I nod.

"When Anna was four days old, she got the hiccups.

She'd had them a lot in utero, so it made sense that she'd get them a lot in real life, too, but this was the first time, and they were big, hurty hiccups, and she cried. I cried, too. Hard. Because how the hell was I going to ever send her to preschool, let alone middle school, where she was going to get the shit kicked out of her by life, if I couldn't deal with her having hiccups? Heath came in and found the two of us, me losing my shit, and he freaked out, of course, because he hadn't ever seen me cry before—if you can believe that—"

"I can believe it," I say. "Only girl in a family with five brothers."

"Right," she says, smiling. "So I try to explain what's wrong, and I'm sobbing and wailing, 'I can't do this! I can't do this!' Sound familiar?" she asks.

Something tight loosens in my chest, and I realize how scared I've been. Not just for the last few minutes, but for a while now. Scared that the only thing I *really* wanted—not just felt like I should want—is the one thing I can't have.

"He said, 'You can do this, Amanda.'"

"Damn," I say. "That's exactly what I should have said. Fuck me."

"Well, no," Amanda says. "Because I threw a shoe at his head, and he had to have twelve stitches."

I wince.

"My point is that strong women break big. And Mari? She's strong. Like ox."

I make a face at her.

"Like very pretty feminine ox," she amends.

"She *is* strong," I say. "But why do you say that?"

"Lucy told me she heard you're going to be exhibiting your photos at the Weirhauser Gallery."

My mouth falls open. Somehow, in the headlong gallop and muddle of the last few days, I'd forgotten completely about my photos. About the meeting that Kelsey had set up with Don Weirhauser, about the offer he'd made to exhibit my work, about the contract I'd signed, and the date he'd set for the opening.

"Your photos—they're phenomenal, Kane—but we all knew that. We just didn't think about what all that talent *meant*. But she did. And she convinced you to think about it, too. If she could get you to own that side of you... well, then she's a hero to me."

"She is a hero," I say, and suddenly I'm swamped in memories, like photos thrown one after another on a coffee table: the way she looked, alone at the bar in Vegas, like a bright light in a dark room; the sight of her stepping out of the Airstream that first day at the ranchland office, already big with our baby; the way she quietly stood back and let me see the world through my camera on our trip; the sound of her cries in the quiet RV; the strength in her hand and the fierce will in her eyes as she bore down and brought Zara into this world.

"She's everything."

Oh my God, I'm an idiot.

"I have to go back inside. I have to tell her she *can* do this. That we can do it together. I can't believe I walked out on her!"

I try to pull myself up out of the driver's seat, but she grabs my arm again. "Kane. Wait."

This time I don't fight.

She smiles wryly. "Honestly, K, it was a good choice. If you'd stayed in that room, all that was going to happen was you were going to get a shoe thrown at your head. Also— how much sleep did *you* get last night?"

"A couple of hours," I admit, and as I say it a heaviness falls in my chest, a fatigue so intense it almost knocks me off my feet. I sink back down.

"Right. So—you're not at your best?"

That's an understatement. "No."

"So just—stay here a sec. Take a deep breath. Give her a few more minutes. I think Lucy's going to give her a pep talk and make sure she gets some sleep, and *then* you can talk to her. By then I'm guessing she'll already know for herself that she *can*. In the meantime, maybe you can lie down for a few minutes in the Airstream? Just a few. Lucy and I have this all under control."

She helps me to my feet. I'm so tired, I don't even resist. I just let her steer me to the Airstream and tuck me into the bed.

My eyes are already closing, but there's something—a couple of somethings—I know I need to do. *Before* I can tell Mari anything.

Because before I tell her I know who she is, I have to make sure I know who I am.

"I need two favors," I tell Amanda.

"Anything," she says fondly. "Shoot."

I tell her the first one. She listens carefully, then says, "Okay. Might be a tall order, but I'm on it."

"Just—do your best."

"And I need to talk to Gabe."

She squints at me. "Wait, what? What do you mean you need to talk to Gabe?"

"I need you to get him out here to talk to me."

"Like, you're *summoning* Gabe? Our Gabe? Our bossy-ass big brother."

"Yup," I say. "I'm fucking summoning Gabe."

"Huh," Amanda says. "Huh. I like that. I like the big brass balls, Kane."

"I'm still the boy next door," I say, muzzily.

"You just keep telling yourself that, babe," she says, and pats my head fondly.

That's the last thing I remember before I'm out like a light.

40

MARI

I lunge from the couch. "I have to go after him. I have to tell him I didn't mean it!"

"Shhh," Lucy says, and she gently eases me back onto the couch. "Amanda's got him. She'll tell him."

"What if he doesn't believe her? What if he thinks—I kept saying I wasn't sure if I could stay—what if this time, he isn't willing to give me another chance?"

I can hear the near hysteria in my voice.

Barb is standing quietly, watching us. Not saying anything. I wonder what she thinks now of this madwoman who is the mother of her granddaughter. But her face is nonjudgmental. Soothingly gentle and kind. It makes me feel a little calmer.

"This is Kane we're talking about," Lucy says. "He's got the biggest heart of anyone I've ever met. And he doesn't make snap decisions. Deep breaths. You're not your best self right now. Calm down, and then you can talk to Kane." She pats my arm and smiles at me. "You know what I did when Willow was four days old? I got in the car and started driving away."

My mouth falls open.

"Yup. I got two miles before I pulled over, burst into tears, and drove home again. I like to think that was as far as that umbilical cord was going to stretch."

"But you? *You* tried to leave?"

She shakes her head. "I never would have done it. Not in a thousand years. And neither would you."

I pull my knees up, hugging them to myself. "How do you know? How can you know that if even I don't know it?"

"I think you do know it."

"My mother left. How do you know I won't do that?"

Lucy sits down on the couch beside me. "How old were you?"

"Twelve."

"Oof. That's rough."

"She hated holding still. Still does. Always has to be on the move. That's how I've been, too."

"You've been holding still for a while now," Lucy says quietly. "How long have you been in Rush Creek? Almost two months? That's a lot of chances to leave if you wanted to leave. And yet you're still here. Are you hating every minute of it?"

Tears pour down my cheeks. "No," I say. "I'm loving every minute of it. Except maybe the last couple of hours."

She smiles. "Understandably. Look. I used to hate small towns. I didn't think I could ever live in one again. But love changes you. It anchors you. It holds you and buoys you and makes things possible that weren't possible before. There's a lot of love here. Kane's, and Zara's, and mine—"

"And mine."

I'd almost forgotten Barb was there. I turn to find her smiling tenderly at me.

I sob for a few minutes while they both wait patiently. Barb finds a box of tissues and hands them to me, one at a time, and when I start to rise to throw away the ones I've used, she holds out her hand.

I protest, but she gently wrestles them out of my grip and makes them disappear.

"How about you get some sleep?" Lucy asks. "While Z's asleep?"

"Z," I say. "You gave her a nickname."

"Oh, shit, I'm sorry, that was presumptuous."

"No. I like it."

"I'll watch out for her. You sleep. And we'll wake you up when she needs to nurse again. She fed a lot earlier, right? I bet you'll get two hours."

She leads me into the bedroom and tucks me in. And she's right. I fall asleep right away, and I sleep hard, harder than I have since Z was born.

When I wake up, Lucy's gone. Amanda sits in a rocking chair on the front porch, doing something that looks very involved on her laptop, and Barb is on the couch, holding Zara, who's just starting to stir. I feel like a different woman. Still exhausted, but calm.

And sheepish.

"I'm so sorry," I tell Barb. "That was—"

"That was par for the course," she says, and pats the

couch next to her. "I have something else to say to you, sweetheart."

"Of course."

I brace myself for a lecture. Kane's her baby, and she probably wants to make sure I'm not going to hurt him. Or maybe she wants to make sure I see a therapist about my post-partum stuff—which, I'll be honest, I should probably do. I make a mental note to call someone once Barb and Amanda leave, and maybe set up a couple of check-in visits.

"Not having your mom around when you have a baby is tough. I know, because mine died seven months before Gabe was born. Having him without her was the second hardest thing I've ever done."

I don't have to ask what the hardest was. Kane told me about her fight with breast cancer after her husband's death.

But now I understand why she's being so awesome. She sees herself in me, somewhere, somehow. We couldn't be more different—the sturdy, well-rooted Pacific North-western grandma versus me... a butterfly who never lands.

Except I seem to have landed, haven't I?

She touches my cheek. "So if you need anything —*anything*—please reach out to me. I can come over here even if it's just to give you and Z a big hug. Or hold her while she naps. Obviously I'm talented at that." She gestures at my sleeping daughter.

"I don't want to... be a bother," I whisper.

She tilts her head. "Oh, hon. That's what it's really about, isn't it? Being afraid you're a bother. That we'll only tolerate you if you're easy and no trouble." She purses her lips. "I imagine that's the hardest thing for someone who got left behind. Believing that you're lovable—no matter what."

I burst into tears again.

Because she's right.

She's shaking her head. "But all you have to do is let Kane prove it to you. Let all of us prove it to you. That's all. Just hold still and let us love you and Zara. Think you can do that?"

I can't actually speak.

The tissues come out again, and in the interim she's found an empty paper bag for the used ones. She knew this would happen again, and she was ready.

When I'm just hiccupy, she touches my hair, pushing it back from where it's stuck in the tears on my face.

Just then, Zara gives a squawk. I take the opportunity of there no longer being a sleeping baby between us to give Barb a gigantic hug.

"Thank you," I say. "Just—thank you. And yes. I can do that. I can let you love us."

She beams at me.

"Let me just change her," she says. "And then I'll give her to you."

"You don't have to do that. It's bad enough that you had to throw out my used tissues—"

She gives me a stern look. "Mari," she says. "I'm only going to say this once, but I want you to listen carefully. I know it's not the same as having your mom around, but I have big mom energy and I'm not afraid to use it. Used tissues are nothing, and neither is newborn poop. Let me change the goddamned diaper."

In that moment I know for sure what I've been

suspecting for weeks now: There's nothing fiercer or better than Wilder love.

"Barb," I ask. "Can I ask you and Lucy and Amanda for one more favor?"

She grins.

"Absolutely."

41

MARI

After I nurse Zara, Barb takes her again, and she and Lucy convince me to take another nap. Kane, it turns out, is having some kind of super-intense business conversation with Gabe in the Airstream, so I can't apologize and beg his forgiveness yet.

It's dark when I wake up, and I'm not alone in the bed. Kane is curled up behind me, an arm draped over me. I peek over and see Zara, sound asleep in the bassinet.

Kane stirs, startles, then says, "Hey."

I roll so I'm facing him. He looks wary, a little worried, but not anything bigger. I feel a rush of relief.

We both open our mouths at the same time, but I get my words out first. "Hey. I'm, um, really, really sorry."

He shakes his head. "No. I'm sorry. I shouldn't have walked out. I should have stayed and talked about it." The corner of his mouth pulls up. "But Amanda says it's good I didn't, because when Heath tried that when Anna was four days old? Amanda threw a shoe at his head, and he had to have stitches."

That makes me laugh. It sounds rusty and creaky, but it's definitely a laugh, and it transforms the quirk of Kane's mouth into a full-on smile. "I guess compared to that I'm pretty tame," I say.

"Yeah," he says. "It just freaked me out. Because—"

I touch his cheek, stubbly from days of rare showers and no time for shaving. "I know why. And I'm so sorry. I didn't mean it like it sounded. I want to stay." I take a deep breath. I think of what Barb said, about how the hardest thing for someone who's been left is letting herself be loved. And I know exactly what I need to do.

"I love you."

It's the first time I've said it to him, and it's not easy. The last person I said it to drove out of my life in an RV and never came back. After that, I didn't much want to say it— or feel it. But Kane hasn't given me a choice, and neither have the rest of the Wilders. And hell yes, I love them for it.

"I love you, too," he says. "I didn't say it sooner because I thought it might freak you out."

"Yeah. Probably would have. A little. But I'm not freaked out now. Your mom pointed out that it's hard, when you've gotten left behind, to let people love you. She said—"

The tears start again. Apparently this is just how it's gonna be for a while. Okay. I can live with that.

"She said all I have to do is stay put and let you and the rest of your family love me and Zara."

He smiles and cups a hand around my cheek. He leans in and kisses me, soft, warm, and sure. His tongue sweeps into my mouth, claiming me, and despite the fact that the key organs still hurt like hell, I feel the faintest stirrings of need for him.

But that, obviously, will have to wait.

When he pulls back, heat in his eyes—that will, unfortunately, also have to wait—he says, "She's right. That's all you have to do. And I promise to do my part. In fact, I couldn't not love you if I tried. I mean," he says quickly, "that wasn't a challenge."

I giggle.

"And you can do it a day at a time, too, you know. Just like we've done these last couple of months. No big promises, no huge commitments, just you, me, and Zara. You stay, and it turns out okay, just like it has all along. You good with that?"

"Yeah," I say. "I'm super good with that."

"But my mom left one thing out. An important thing. There will be days, like this one, when it feels like you can't. And that's okay, too. If you wake up in the morning and you don't feel like you can stay put?"

My heart pounds when he says it. I don't want him to paint that picture now. I want to rest in his assurance that it won't happen, that day by day by day we can string together months, years, the rest of our lives together, surrounded by his amazing family and all the love they can't help giving.

But he doesn't say exactly what I thought he was going to. Instead, he grabs his phone from the nightstand and starts swiping around and tapping.

He holds it up so I can see the screen.

It's a listing for an Airstream classic. A bigger one than mine. My eyes flick to his face, trying to understand what he's telling me, then back to the listing. The classic has been renovated and revamped for living with small children, with bunks that can be converted to use as toddler beds or even cribs. It's made for seeing the country with little ones in tow.

My eyebrows raise—because apparently, great minds think alike.

"Amanda made an offer on it," Kane says. "And they accepted it."

I'm laughing now. "You're kidding me!"

His brows draw together. "What's so funny?" He sounds a little hurt.

"I told Amanda I wanted to sell my Airstream. And you—you told her you wanted to buy a bigger one?"

We look at each other, then burst out laughing.

"Do you think she…?"

He taps out a text to her.

"Yep," he says. "She offered your Airstream in trade for this one," he says. "She got us both what we wanted." He shakes his head in admiration.

I look at his dear, beautiful face—the hard lines and steely bone structure all Wilder, the tenderness all Kane. "What *I* wanted was for you to know I'd never run," I tell him.

The creases in his forehead deepen, his eyes soft and warm on me. "And what I wanted was for you to know that if you ever needed to run, I'd go with you."

My breath catches in my throat.

He smiles. "I also told Gabe that I was going to need more time off to travel for my photography work, and that in lieu of doing igloo camping and snowshoe cocoa trips, I'd be happy to incorporate nature photography lessons into any other Wilder trip. He was pissed about the time-off thing, but whatever. Gabe's always hot under the collar about something."

"You did that?" Because it's still new to me to imagine that someone could change their life around to make room for me in it. The last person I loved… well, she couldn't—or wouldn't, which amounted to the same thing.

But that was her loss, wasn't it?

That was her fucking loss.

I straighten up and put my hands on my hips, a silent acknowledgment that it's time to stop hiding from love because of what she couldn't give me.

Kane wipes a stray tear off my cheek. "After you told me your life was on the road, I kept seeing it as *your* either-or. Either you stayed or you went. And meanwhile, I had to keep being who I've always been—the peacemaker, the boy next door, the easy brother. And there was nothing I could do about it. I'd trapped myself in that version of the story."

He strokes a hand down one side of his face. I can hear the rough of his palm on the days of stubble he hasn't had time to shave away.

"Then I Googled the quote on your bracelet. The Tolkien quote. Do you know the whole thing?"

I shake my head.

He pushes a strand of hair off my forehead.

All that is gold does not glitter, Not all those who wander are lost; The old that is strong does not wither, Deep roots are not reached by the frost.

"Oh!" I say.

"Right? It doesn't mean at *all* what I thought it meant, either."

"Deep roots are not reached by the frost," I quote.

He nods, a wry smile tugging up one corner of his

mouth, putting a dimple there. "And I realized that my whole idea that it had to be one way or the other—stay put or go—was absurd and predicated on the idea that the only way I can be the man I'm supposed to be is by doing exactly what my brothers think they need me to do. By working full time for Wilder. And that's just not true. In fact, the only way I can be the man I want to be is to change the way I'm doing things so I can spend time on my photography—and, even more so—be with you and Zara."

I'm crying again, of course, as he wraps his arms around me, kissing away the tears. Our mouths find each other, a long, sweet reunion—until Zara fusses in the bassinet next to me. Then Kane gets up, changes her, and brings her to me, and we lie in the bed together for a long time, being a family.

EPILOGUE
KANE—MANY MONTHS LATER

"I had no idea you were this talented…"

"Congratulations…"

"These are *amazing*…"

I shake hands, receive smiles and kudos, accept claps on the back and lots of hugs from friends and family. And it's—

Well, it feels pretty damn good.

I have to say, right now, it feels like it'll never get old. Being the center of attention. Not the Wilder who does whatever needs to be done, the one who holds back and forgets his own pizza order, but the Wilder who kicked some ass, took some names, and is currently attending his own official opening at an art gallery.

My photographs line both rooms of the Weirhauser gallery, mostly black and whites, framed in simple black frames. There are small descriptions with prices that I helped the gallery owner write. He wanted to set the prices about three times as high as I thought was reasonable, and he won the fight. Despite that, all but a few now have red *sold* dots on them.

Everyone's here. My mother and brothers, their wives and girlfriends, my sister and her husband and their kids—adorable in their best clothes—and our extended family, which seems to grow, delightfully, every year, and now includes Mari's friends Arlene and John, who came from California for the opening. Even the Wilder Adventures "new guy," Bear Warden, is here, which was pretty standup of him. Bear's a celebrity wilderness forager-slash-chef who's here for the summer to do a series of special events. Gabe brought him in, and so far he seems like a great fit.

Mari's mom's not here, but I think that's okay. Recently, she FaceTimed Mari to apologize for dropping off the face of the earth this year and suggested they get together near Yellowstone National Park's east entrance later this month.

Mari said no. She said it wasn't a good time and that she had a job to finish up in Bend, which is absolutely true. She's been finding lots of local work, plus more jobs within a night or two of home. We've even taken a few trips with Zara in tow in the new and completely kickass Airstream.

Mari sounded calm on the FaceTime call, and when she hung up, she shrugged and said, "There's a Wilder dinner scheduled for that night and I'm not gonna miss that so she can make me feel shitty again."

Mari freaked out—her words, not mine—twice more after that first time she and I were so sleep deprived that our family had to intervene. But in both cases, she got right on the phone, called Lucy and Amanda and my mom, took a nice long nap, and got herself back on track. She's been seeing a therapist ever since, too—her idea—and she says it's been incredibly helpful, not just for keeping an eye on her post-partum moods, but also to help her work through some of her feelings about her mom.

I look over at Mari. She's standing a little distance away, admiring a photo of an old accordion at the Sluice Box. Zara's on her front, sleeping in the carrier, with one of Mari's hands cupped protectively over her little butt.

Every time I look over and see that, something in the middle of my chest goes as gooey as a campfire marshmallow. My girls.

I go stand next to them.

"What do you think?"

"I think they're beautiful," she says. "I think you're amazing. And I'm so, so proud of you."

"Don't they look great?" Don Weirhauser asks, coming up behind her. "I fell in love with them at first glance. And sales are going so well that I'd like to do another exhibit later this year." He drifts away to talk to Bear, who's been standing for several minutes in front of a photograph of Black Magic Canyon.

Mari looks around the room. "So those red dots are —*sold* dots?"

"Yup."

"Holy *shit*, Kane!"

"I know. It's all going into Zara's college account."

"College," she murmurs. "God. Let me get her out of diapers first." Her forehead wrinkles. "Wait. Who bought the one of me?" she demands.

There are several of her, but the one she's referring to is the naked, pregnant photo. True, one hand is wrapped modestly across her breasts and the other discreetly covers her sex, but let's face it—there's plenty of Mari left on full display, and I'll be the first to admit it—that photo's not art to me. It's pure, straight up, Mari-porn. Which is why...

"I marked that one sold before I displayed it," I admit. "I couldn't stand the thought of anyone other than me getting to own a photo of you naked."

She smiles. "I wouldn't have minded."

"I would have."

Her smile gets bigger.

My family starts drifting over, first Amanda, then Easton, Rachel, Lucy, Jessa, and Hanna. They all congratulate me—not for the first time—and reveal their true colors by trying to figure out if Zara's awake and if they can hold her.

Answer: no, and hell no, because if I've learned anything this year, it's never to wake a sleeping baby.

Don Weirhauser has just slapped a red *sold* dot on the Black Magic Canyon photo that Bear was standing in front of.

"Well, hell, that was decent of him," I say.

"Kane," Amanda chides. "He didn't do it to be nice. He did it because your photos kick ass."

"Yeah, yeah, yeah." I'm still trying to get used to this idea.

"But Bear *is* super nice."

That's Hanna, and to my surprise, her observation is accompanied by a deep blush.

Lucy smiles at her friend. "Does that have anything to do with why I've never seen you wearing that top before?"

I hadn't noticed till she mentioned it, but Hanna isn't wearing her usual t- or sweatshirt. She's wearing a red blouse-like thing that might even be described, by those in the know, as "cute."

"He's been totally great on the trips." Hanna's tone is neutral, but the blush deepens.

Easton scuffs his shoe against the floor, my eye drawn to it and then up to the frown on his face.

"He's obviously not local," Mari says, her tone teasing. "And he's not married or engaged."

"Nope," Rachel says. "Or if he is, it's the best kept secret in celebrity-chefdom."

"He's available," Jessa teases.

"Stop!" Hanna says. "You *guys!*"

With a roll of her eyes and a cross of her arms, Hanna harumphs off.

Amanda has been surprisingly quiet. I turn to her. "I don't hear any snarky commentary from you, sister dearest."

"Huh," she says, a smirk tugging up one corner of her mouth. I know that look. My sister has intel the rest of us don't have... and she's going to milk it for all it's worth. "Rumor has it... Bear is Hanna's date tonight."

"Seriously?" I ask.

Amanda pointedly casts her eyes across the room, and we all try to look that direction while pretending we're not. We all love Hanna, and I think it's fair to say we're all rooting for whatever will make her happy—and kind of dying to find out what that is.

What I see is Bear standing in front of another of my photos, examining it with that same overwhelming inten-sity that he gave the one he just purchased. Hanna stands next to him, also looking at the photo. Their pinky fingers almost touch.

"Did she just *Bridgerton*-art-gallery-scene him?" Lucy demands.

"I think she did," Rachel says, amused.

"What's going on?" Amanda demands.

For some reason, we all look at Easton. "What makes you think I know?" He lifts one shoulder in a classic Easton nonchalant shrug.

But there's something in his face that doesn't match the gesture. I study him for a moment more.

His eyes are on Hanna.

He crosses and uncrosses his arms. "I'd better..." he says.

But he doesn't finish the sentence. He just walks away, toward the exit.

"Oh, my," Amanda says.

"Huh," Mari says slowly beside me. "This should be—very, very interesting."

Amanda touches her nose. Points to Mari.

"I knew I liked you, sister," she says.

AUTHOR'S NOTE AND ACKNOWLEDGMENTS

Author's Note: *A Little Wilder* is a book about choices. I know that Mari gave careful thought to her options, that in her fictional world—the world I want to live in—they all felt possible and accessible. She could have, and would have, made different decisions if she had needed to, and still found her happily ever after. Above all, her decisions were hers to make, as they always should be.

Acknowledgments: Readers, I love you. You have made writing this series a complete delight. Thank you for coming along with me on this Wild(er) ride!

Thank you so much to my early readers, Christina Hovland, Dylann Crush, Brenda St. John Brown, and Rachel Grant. Thank you for taking time away from your own stories to help make this book the best it could be. Special thanks to Eliza Jones for being my "cold" reader— the one who gets to tell me whether someone entering the series with this book can make sense of the Wilder madness.

Writing books is strange work, and I owe my enjoyment of it to both my readers and my author friends. Huge thanks also to the author friends who support me on a regular basis—Audrey, Cheryl, Dylann, Megan, Christy, Brenda, Christine, Gwen, Rachel, Kate, Kris, Karen, Susannah, Claire, and many, many more, including but not limited to the authors of the Corner of Smart and Sexy, RAM Rom Com, Wide for the Win, Awesome Babes for Good Things, and my ongoing newsletter swaps.

Thank you to my agent, Emily Sylvan Kim, and my sub rights agent, Tina Shen!

Thank you, Sarah Sarai! I love working with you. Little did you know that your efforts this time would stray into tech troubleshooting—thank you for bearing with me on the strange case of the just-plain-wrong open quote marks! And thanks for that insight into a famous actor's improbable middle name and the warning about my inadvertent crib of *The Omen*... I depend on you for these sorts of things.

Thank you, XPresso Book Tours, especially Giselle, for the release blitz!

Hugs and kisses for my not-author friends who support my imaginary worlds with so much love and patience: Aimee, Chelsea, Darya, Ellen, Gail, Jess, Julia, Kathy, Lauren, Molly, Soomie, and Tracey.

To BellGirl and BellBoy, you are the very best of all the people who have come before you—I am so proud of you and so blessed to have you in my life.

Mr. Bell: Thank you for arriving in my life like a romance hero in a meet cute; I always knew the stories were true but it sure as heck makes them easier to write when I have my own HEA. I love you.

Any errors of fact or insensitivity relating to representation are mine and mine alone. If you note any, please let me know so I can apologize and learn to be better.

ALSO BY SERENA BELL

Wilder Adventures

Make Me Wilder

Walk on the Wilder Side

Wilder With You

A Little Wilder

Wilder at Last

Under One Roof

Do Over

Head Over Heels

Sleepover

Returning Home

Hold On Tight

Can't Hold Back

To Have and to Hold

Holding Out

Tierney Bay

So Close

So True

So Good (2022)

So Right (2023)

New York Glitz

Still So Hot!

Hot & Bothered

Standalone

Turn Up the Heat

ABOUT THE AUTHOR

USA Today bestselling author Serena Bell writes contemporary romance with heat, heart, and humor. A former journalist, Serena has always believed that everyone has an amazing story to tell if you listen carefully, and you can often find her scribbling in her tiny garret office, main-lining chocolate and bringing to life the tales in her head.

Serena's books have earned many honors, including a RITA finalist spot, an RT Reviewers' Choice Award, Apple Books Best Book of the Month, and Amazon Best Book of the Year for Romance.

When not writing, Serena loves to spend time with her college-sweetheart husband and two hilarious kiddos—all of whom are incredibly tolerant not just of Serena's imaginary friends but also of how often she changes her hobbies and how passionately she embraces the new ones. These days, it's stand-up paddle boarding, board-gaming, meditation, and long walks with good friends.

www.ingramcontent.com/pod-product-compliance
Lightning Source LLC
Chambersburg PA
CBHW060912190726
48286CB00002B/479